William Munk

The life of Sir Henry Halford

William Munk

The life of Sir Henry Halford

ISBN/EAN: 9783337269241

Printed in Europe, USA, Canada, Australia, Japan

Cover: Foto ©Raphael Reischuk / pixelio.de

More available books at **www.hansebooks.com**

THE LIFE OF
SIR HENRY HALFORD, Bart.

SIR HENRY HALFORD, BART. G.C.H. M.D. F.R.S.

THE LIFE OF

SIR HENRY HALFORD, Bart.

G.C.H., M.D., F.R.S.

PRESIDENT OF THE ROYAL COLLEGE OF PHYSICIANS

PHYSICIAN TO GEORGE III., GEORGE IV., WILLIAM IV., AND

TO HER MAJESTY QUEEN VICTORIA

BY

WILLIAM MUNK, M.D., F.S.A.

FELLOW AND LATE VICE-PRESIDENT OF THE ROYAL COLLEGE
OF PHYSICIANS OF LONDON

LONDON
LONGMANS, GREEN AND CO.
AND NEW YORK
1895

TO

SIR JOHN RUSSELL REYNOLDS, BART.,

M.D., F.R.S.

PRESIDENT OF THE ROYAL COLLEGE OF PHYSICIANS

AND

PHYSICIAN TO THE QUEEN'S HOUSEHOLD

ETC. ETC.

THIS LIFE OF

ONE OF THE MOST DISTINGUISHED OF HIS PREDECESSORS

IN THE CHAIR OF THE ROYAL COLLEGE OF PHYSICIANS

IS RESPECTFULLY DEDICATED

BY

THE AUTHOR

PREFACE

" THE conduct of a physician," to use Sir Henry Halford's own words, " on whom is fixed the only hope of saving life, and on whom the dying look often rests, before the eye is closed for ever, may fairly be thought interesting to every hearer."* Equally may it be thought so to every reader; and this is likely to be especially the case when the physician has held an exceptionally prominent and distinguished position before the public and among his professional brethren. Such was emphatically true of Sir Henry Halford. With the full accord of his colleagues, he was, for twenty-four years, president of the College of Physicians, and as such the acknowledged head of the medical profession in this country. He was, too, physician to four of our successive sovereigns—to George III., George IV., William IV., and Queen Victoria: and he was repeatedly called into medical

* " Essays and Orations read and delivered at the Royal College of Physicians." Third edition, London, 1842, p. iv.

attendance on all the royal dukes and on all the princesses.

The life and conduct of one so distinguished cannot but be interesting, both in itself and as a contribution to the social history of his time.

Sir Henry Halford has been dead for more than half a century. In that space of time circumstances, which at a prior period would be rightly regarded as private, become conventionally matters of history, and thenceforth are so regarded and treated. It is believed that the time has arrived when the events in which Sir Henry Halford bore a prominent part fall within the domain of history ; and therefore that his life may now be written.

I have undertaken to write it at the request, formally expressed to me by the College of Physicians, that I should do so.

In doing it, I have striven to place myself *in* the period of which I am speaking, and *out* of that in which I am actually writing. A due degree of candour is needed, alike by the author and the reader, in judging between the conventional opinions of the present time and of those which then prevailed. We have to judge of men according to their actual environments, and I have sought to place Sir Henry Halford, his person-

ality and character, in due relation to his contemporaries and surroundings, and to the spirit
of the time in which he lived.

I am indebted to Sir Henry St. John Halford,
Bart., the grandson of the physician, for the
freest use of all the letters, diaries, pocket and
note books, engagement and fee books, that have
been preserved and are now at Wistow. Among
these are some notes made by Sir Henry
Halford, the second baronet, who at one time
contemplated writing a Life of his father. But
he made little progress with it. His notes, however, have furnished me with many facts, not
otherwise recorded, derived from conversations
with his father, and with other members of the
Vaughan family.

WILLIAM MUNK.

40 FINSBURY SQUARE,
Sept. 24, 1895.

CONTENTS

CHAPTER I

The Vaughans of Leicester—William Vaughan, M.D., of Colchester and London—Ann Newton, of Romford, his wife—Sir Henry Newton, master of St. Katherine's Hospital by the Tower, and judge in the Court of Admiralty—Rev. Henry Vaughan, vicar of Leominster and master of the Leominster grammar school—Henry Vaughan, of Leominster, surgeon—James Vaughan, M.D., of Leicester—His sons: James Vaughan—Henry Vaughan, the future Sir Henry Halford, Bart.—The Right Hon. Sir John Vaughan, a privy councillor and a justice of the Common Pleas—The very Rev. Peter Vaughan, D.D., warden of Merton College, Oxford, and dean of Chester—William Welby Vaughan—The Right Hon. Sir Charles Vaughan, a privy councillor and minister to the United States of America—The Rev. Edward Thomas Vaughan, vicar of St. Martin's, Leicester   .   . pp. 1-15

CHAPTER II

Henry Vaughan, subsequently Sir Henry Halford, Bart.—His birth, and education at Rugby school and at Christ Church, Oxford—His degrees in arts—Studying medicine at Edinburgh, and its practice at Leicester—Proceeds bachelor of medicine at Oxford and begins to practise physic at Leicester—Graduates doctor of medicine of Oxford and settles as physician at Scarborough—Consults Sir George Baker on his chances of success as a physician in London—Settles in London, is elected physician to the Middlesex Hospital, and admitted a fellow of the College of Physicians   .   .   .   . pp. 16-24

CHAPTER III

His professional life to 1809—Created physician-extraordinary to
the King—His marriage—Delivers the Harveian oration of
1800—Illness and death of Georgina, Duchess of Devonshire
—Its effect on the reputation and practice of Dr. Vaughan—
Charles James Fox—His medical contemporaries at this
time: Sir George Baker, Bart.; Dr. Henry Revell-Reynolds;
Sir Walter Farquhar, Bart.—Dr. Vaughan's business and
emoluments—Earnings of London physicians from Radcliffe
downwards—Medical fees for long journeys and special
services—Reduction of fees for distant journeys on the
establishment of railways . . . . . PP. 25-45

CHAPTER IV

Succeeds to the Halford estate of Wistow in Leicestershire—
Changes his name by Act of Parliament from Vaughan to
Halford—Created a baronet—Called, along with Dr. Matthew
Baillie, into medical attendance on the Princess Amelia at
Windsor—Is appointed physician-in-ordinary to the Prince
of Wales, and physician-in-ordinary to George III.—Sir
Gilbert Blane's expedition to Walcheren and Sir Henry
Halford's view of the remuneration due to him for his services
—His opinion of vaccination—Its failure in the case of a son
of the Earl Grosvenor—Opening of the coffin of Charles I.
in the vault of King Henry VIII. at St. George's, Windsor,
with a view to its identification—His report of the proceedings—Death of Lady Denbigh and Sir Henry's succession to
Wistow—Its history in connection with the Halford family—
His alterations, extension and improvements of the hall,
grounds, and estate generally—His life at Wistow pp. 46-66

CHAPTER V

Sir Henry Halford from 1820 to his death in 1844—Elected
president of the Royal College of Physicians—Becomes a
trustee of the British Museum—Death of his friend and
colleague, Dr. Baillie—Baillie's trust in Sir Henry Halford
as friend and as physician, reciprocated in full, by
Halford—His eulogium on Baillie from the chair of the
College of Physicians—Proposes the erection of a bust in
the college to his honour and memory—Threatened advent

of Asiatic cholera to this country in 1831—Halford consulted
by the government—A Board of Health instituted, but super-
seded by a Central Board of Health—Death of Lady Halford
—Sir Henry admitted to an ad eundem degree at Cambridge
—Letter from the chancellor of the University, the Duke of
Gloucester—Death of two distinguished London physicians,
Dr. Maton and Dr. Pelham Warren—The death of Mr.
Lockley—Sir Henry Halford's statement of the circumstances
of that event—Sir Henry Halford's devotion to classical
subjects and to the composition of Latin poetry—His
" Nugæ Metricæ "—His decline of health, last illness, and
death—Buried at Wistow—Incription to his memory there—
His will   .   .   .   . pp. 67-100

CHAPTER VI

Sir Henry Halford and the College of Physicians—The college
in Warwick Lane, Newgate Street—Elected president of the
college—Applies himself to the removal of the college to the
West End—Obtains from the Crown a grant of the site in
Pall Mall East, on which the college now stands—Building
of the present college from the designs of Sir Robert Smirke
—A high honour conferred on the college by George IV.—
Dr. Southey admitted a fellow of the college by command of
the King—A bust of Sir Henry Halford voted by some of
the fellows in recognition of his eminent services to the
college—Opening of the new college—Distinguished persons
present on that occasion—Sir Henry defrays the expenses of
the opening—Evening meetings at the college—Their object
and success—Sir Henry Halford's communications at these
meetings—He encounters some unpopularity with junior
fellows of the college—Change in the constitution of the
college and in sequel thereto a lowering of the culture,
attainments and social position of the English physician—
Sir Henry delivers the Harveian oration of 1835—His
nominations to the fellowship, speciali gratiâ . pp. 101-134

CHAPTER VII

Sir Henry Halford and the Royal Family—Is appointed physician-
extraordinary to the King—Is called into medical attendance
on the Duke and Duchess of Gloucester—Consulted by the
Duke of Kent; by the Duke and Duchess of Cumberland—

Along with Dr. Baillie is placed in medical charge of the Princess Amelia; her illness and death—George III.: his command to Sir Henry Halford to assume the medical charge of his Majesty if occasion should arise for it—The King's attack, long illness, and death—Queen Charlotte's illness and death—The Duke of York, his last illness, and circumstances attending it—Correspondence with Sir Herbert Taylor—The Duke's death—Grant of armorial augmentations and supporters to Sir Henry Halford—He is appointed physician to the Prince of Wales—Sir Matthew Tierney, Bart.—Sir Henry appointed physician-in-ordinary to George IV.—The King's illness immediately after his accession to the throne; his habitual state of health during the ten years of his reign; his last illness and death—Sir Henry Halford's vindication of the bulletins then issued and of the conduct generally of the physicians—His exposition of the rules to guide the conduct of physicians, in their intercourse with patients under mortal or dangerous diseases—Presentation to Sir Henry Halford by the Royal Family of a splendid clock in testimony of gratitude for his professional services to the Princess Amelia, the Queen Charlotte, George III., the Duke of York, and George IV.—Appointed first physician to William IV., who confers on him the Grand Cross of Hanover—Last illness of William IV.—Sir Henry Halford and Dr. Chambers called into attendance: circumstances attending it—The King's death—Sir Henry Halford emphatically the friend of the Royal Family—His office of actual medical attendant on the sovereign terminates.

pp. 135–195

CHAPTER VIII

Sir Henry Halford much given to letter-writing—His letters from members of the Royal Family—The Duke of Cumberland and King of Hanover—The Duke of Kent—The Duke of Cambridge, Viceroy of Hanover—The Duke of Sussex—The Princess Augusta—The Princess Mary, Duchess of Gloucester—Mrs. Fitzherbert .   .   .   . pp. 196–218

CHAPTER IX

Sir Henry Halford's correspondents continued—The Marquess Wellesley—The Duke of Wellington—Sir Henry puts into Latin the Duke's acceptance of the offer of the chancellorship of the University of Oxford in 1834—The Duke and

Duchess of Bedford—The Duke of Rutland—Sir Robert Peel,
Bart., suggests an alteration in Sir Henry's Latin translation of
Pope's Epistle to Gay—General Phipps—Lord Grosvenor—
Colonel Grosvenor—Lord Holland—The Duke of Dorset—
Duke of Cleveland—Handsome fee to Sir Henry Halford—
The elder d'Israeli's opinion of Halford—Letter from Sir
Henry Halford to Sir Charles Bell on his discovery of the
functions of the spinal nerves .   .   .   . pp. 219-256

CHAPTER X

Sir Henry Halford's character—His personal appearance—
Portrait by Sir Thomas Lawrence at Wistow, and by H.
Room in 1837—His mental characteristics, natural and
acquired—His habit of fixed attention—Dr. Warren his prototype as a physician—His sketch of Dr. Warren—Sir Henry
essentially a practical bedside physician—His confidence in
the power of nature to cure disease—Influence of mind on
disease ; of hope and of fear—Confidence in the physician—
Sir Henry's treatment of symptoms—Sir Henry sanguine by
nature and hopeful under most circumstances—His innate
shrinking from bodily pain or mental suffering—Influence of
hope in the treatment of disease—Sir Henry Halford's
bearing in the sick chamber—His attainments as a practical
physician as compared with Dr. Baillie—Sir Benjamin
Brodie's opinion of Sir Henry Halford contested—Sir
Henry's scientific knowledge of medicine — His early
recognition of the value of vaccination; of the truth
of Sir Charles Bell's discovery of the functions of the
spinal nerves; of Dr. Prout's views of urinary pathology
and animal chemistry, and of the use of the stethoscope in the diagnosis of disease—His view of disease
essentially practical—The cure of disease the physician's
first object—Sir Henry's powers of diagnosis—A good
classical scholar—Love of Latin poetry—Spoke Latin with
ease and elegance—Fond of society and shone in it—An
excellent host—Himself helpless in money matters—Fond of
horses and dogs—Whist—Sir Henry's weaknesses and
failings—Quick of temper and hasty of speech—His courtly
manners—Effects on himself of his intimate and long connection with the court—His services to the College of
Physicians, the profession, and to his patients—Testimonies
to his character—Attachment and liberality to his father
and brothers .   .   .   . pp. 257-284

PORTRAITS

Sir Henry Halford, Bart., M.D., President of the Royal College of Physicians, from his portrait by Sir Thomas Lawrence at Wistow   .   .   *To face title-page*

Sir Henry Halford, from a drawing by H. Room, in 1837   .   .   .   .   .   .   *To face chapter x. p. 257*

ERRATA

P. 93, lines 17 and 22, and p. 94, line 4, *for* Granville *read* Grenville.

THE LIFE OF

SIR HENRY HALFORD, BART.

CHAPTER I

THE VAUGHANS OF LEICESTER

THE Vaughans of Leicester, or the sons of James Vaughan, M.D., of that town, of whom Sir Henry Halford was one, trace back to another physician —to William Vaughan, a doctor of medicine of Leyden, and, by incorporation on that degree, of Cambridge also, and a fellow of the Royal College of Physicians of London. He practised physic for some years at Colchester, and subsequently for many years in London, and died 4th July, 1712, aged about sixty-four. On the 17th August, 1676, he had married at Romford, Essex, Ann Newton of Romford, spinster, a kinswoman, and apparently a sister of Sir Henry Newton, who was employed during the reign of Queen Anne in certain diplomatic missions to the Grand Duke of Tuscany and the Republic of Genoa, wherein he acquitted himself with much credit.　Sir Henry Newton became afterwards Master of St. Katherine's Hospital by the Tower, and a Judge in the Court of Admiralty.

Dr. William Vaughan had by his wife several children : one of these, Henry, was of Queen's College, Cambridge, and as such proceeded A.M. in 1713.　He received ordination in the Church of England, and after holding the chaplaincy of Ashe's Hospital and of the Haberdashers' Almshouses, both of them in London, was made by his kinsman, Sir Henry Newton the master, Chaplain to St. Katherine's.　He officiated there for several years, until presented by Lord Chancellor Parker to two livings in Herefordshire, those of Leominster and of Aymestry near it.　He was soon after appointed master of the Grammar School of Leominster.　He was an intimate friend of Dean Swift, who used to stay with him at Leominster on his way to Ireland.　Mr. Vaughan died in 1762, aged seventy-five.*

The eldest son of the Rev. Henry Vaughan, vicar of Leominster, was Henry Vaughan of Leominster, surgeon, who was born 19th June,

---

* The youngest daughter of Dr. William Vaughan and sister of the Rev. Henry Vaughan, became the wife of the Rev. James Hodgson, and was the grandmother of the Rev. Francis Hodgson, provost of Eton.

1714, and died 23rd June, 1779, aged sixty-five. He was buried at Leominster. He married Prudence Weston, a Herefordshire lady, and by her was the father, among others, of James Vaughan, M.D., of Leicester.

James Vaughan, M.D., was born at Leominster, and baptized there in 1740. Of his general education there is nothing recorded, but as he is known to have been a competent scholar, and devoted to the classics, he was probably at the Leominster Grammar school, of which his grandfather was then the master. He learnt the rudiments of his future profession from his father, and then as a house pupil, read for some time with Dr. John Wall, a learned and celebrated physician, at Worcester. He went next to Edinburgh, where in due course he graduated Doctor of Medicine in June, 1762. He was admitted an extra-licentiate of College of Physicians of London, 8th September, 1762. Dr. Vaughan then settled at Leicester, where he practised with great reputation and success for about forty years. He lived in a large house at the corner of New Street and Friar Lane, and subsequently at one in the High Street, Leicester. He was physician to the Leicester Infirmary, of which institution he was, in 1771, one of the main founders.

Dr. Vaughan was a physician of no ordinary attainments. Acute perception, accurate observation and a just appreciation of the practically important circumstances of disease, were his medical characteristics, to which were added a well-founded reliance in the efficacy of medicine, and no ordinary skill in its adaptation to the special requirements of the case before him. His doses of medicine are said to have been large, but they were administered with a success which afforded ample proof of their correctness.

Dr. Vaughan married Hester, the second daughter of William Smalley, Esq., alderman of Leicester, by Elizabeth, daughter of Sir Richard Halford, Bart., of Wistow, co. Leicester. He had by her seven sons and one daughter: James, Henry, John, Peter, William Welby, Charles Richard, Edward, Almena Selina.

Dr. Vaughan was a very strict disciplinarian in his family. So ambitious was he for the success of his sons, that he is reported to have said, he had rather follow them to their graves than that they should fail to achieve distinction in their respective callings.

To five of his sons Dr. Vaughan gave the most liberal education. He was himself a competent scholar, and keenly alive to the advantages of

classical knowledge in any of the higher departments of life. When his sons attained the age
at which their education should commence, he had
already acquired a moderate competency ; and he
determined for the future to apply the whole of
his annual professional earnings to their education,
trusting that they would reap the harvest by
success in their respective professions. He
impressed upon them that they would succeed to
nothing at his death, for that all he could spare
for their sakes would be devoted to their education. His sons were educated at Rugby, and
five of them received a complete University education—the four elder at Oxford, the youngest at
Cambridge. The gratitude of his sons for this act
of self-denial and confidence in their exertions was
unbounded ; and Sir Henry Halford, in a biogra-
phical sketch of his brother, Mr. Justice Vaughan,
thus feelingly expressed himself: " All the sons
of the late Dr. Vaughan, of Leicester, acknowledge
with deep and sincere gratitude their father's
generosity, as well as his prudence, in resolving as
he did to lay out the annual produce of his profession in affording them the advantage of a liberal
education, whereby they might be enabled to make
their own fortunes, rather than to accumulate
resources not to be made available for any purposes

of theirs until his death.   He sent four of them, therefore, to Oxford when they had left Rugby school, and the youngest subsequently to Cambridge, and not one of them asked or received assistance from him after he had finished his education and commenced his own efforts to provide for himself.   The success of these brothers in their several callings, with the distinctions acquired by each of them, has abundantly justified their parent's sagacity and his liberality, and we record the fact with pleasure, as furnishing a good and useful example of the result of so much prudence and so generous a self-denial."

It should be added that Dr. Vaughan survived not only to be a witness of the success and eminence of Sir Henry Halford, but to receive from him for many years an annuity of three hundred pounds in augmentation of his own pecuniary resources.   Dr. Vaughan, conscious of his own failing powers, withdrew from the practice of his profession several years before his death.   His memory after a time utterly failed him, and he sank gradually into a state of senile imbecility. He died at Leicester on the 19th August, 1813, in the seventy-fifth year of his age, and was buried at Wistow, where a tablet in the church commemorates him thus :

SACRED TO THE MEMORY OF

JAMES VAUGHAN, M.D., AND OF HESTER HIS WIFE

WHO ARE INTERRED BENEATH THIS TABLET.

JAMES VAUGHAN WAS DESCENDED FROM A RESPECTABLE FAMILY IN

HEREFORDSHIRE,

AND PRACTISED PHYSIC IN LEICESTER ABOUT FORTY YEARS

WITH THAT FACILITY AND SUCCESS WHICH A QUICK PERCEPTION,

A SOUND JUDGMENT,

AND A PERFECT KNOWLEDGE OF THE RESOURCES OF HIS ART WERE

CALCULATED TO COMMAND.

HE DIED AUGUST THE 19TH, 1813, IN THE 75TH YEAR OF HIS AGE.

HESTER VAUGHAN WAS THE SECOND DAUGHTER OF WILLIAM SMALLEY, ESQ.,

OF LEICESTER,

BY ELIZABETH HIS WIFE, DAUGHTER OF SIR RICHARD HALFORD, BART.,

OF THIS PLACE,

AND WAS ONE OF THE GENTLEST AND MOST AMIABLE OF WOMEN.

SHE DIED APRIL THE 2ND, 1791, IN THE 51ST YEAR OF HER AGE.

BY THIS CONNECTION WITH THE HOUSE OF WISTOW AND BY THE KIND

DISTINCTION OF SIR CHARLES HALFORD, BART.,

THE LAST MALE HEIR OF THE HALFORDS,

HENRY, ELDEST SURVIVING SON OF JAMES AND HESTER VAUGHAN,

SUCCEEDED TO

THE POSSESSIONS OF THAT ANCIENT AND LOYAL FAMILY.

A portrait of Dr. Vaughan is in the great hall of the mansion at Wistow, as is also one of his wife.

A few particulars relating to the sons of Dr. Vaughan may be interesting, and are subjoined.

I. James Vaughan, the eldest born, was placed at Rugby School in 1774; but of his progress there, nothing is known. He was matriculated at Balliol College, Oxford, in October, 1783, aged eighteen, but left the university without any degree. In expectation of succeeding to the Wistow estate he was not bred to any profession. Leaving home early he made what was regarded by his family as an imprudent marriage on the 7th June, 1786, to Mary Elizabeth, the eldest daughter of Sir Everard Bucknorth Herne. James Vaughan died 29th May, 1788, in the twenty-third year of his age, and is buried in Heydon Church, Essex.

II. Henry, who became Sir Henry Halford, Bart., and is the subject of the following pages.

III. The Right Hon. Sir John Vaughan, born 11th of February 1769. He was educated at Rugby and at Queen's College, Oxford, but left the university without taking a degree, and then took to the law. Foss, in his " Judges of England," writes thus of him : " Called to the bar in 1791, he chose the Midland Circuit, and by his agreeable manners and good connection speedily succeeded. His advance was rapid : first he was elected recorder of his native place, Leicester, and in 1799 he took the degree of Serjeant-at-Law. During the next twenty-eight years he had an immense business, which he owed less to his legal acquirements than to his fluency of speech, and the energy and pertinacity which he always displayed for his clients. In fact, he was not deeply learned in the science, and knew little of the law of real property. But he was industrious and painstaking, and though his manner was somewhat boisterous, his addresses to the jury were humorous and effective. For his subsequent advances, in 1814 as Solicitor, and in 1816 as Attorney-General to Queen Charlotte; in the same year as King's Serjeant; and lastly, on 24th February, 1827, as a Baron of the Exchequer in the place of Sir Robert Graham, he was no doubt greatly indebted to the influence of his brother, the Royal physician. After sitting in the Exchequer for seven years, he exchanged, on 29th April, 1834, with Sir Edward Alderson into the Common Pleas, and was at the same time honoured with a seat in the Privy Council, where he remained till his sudden death, in September, 1839, of a heart complaint. As a judge, he was much respected for his kind and gentlemanly demeanour, and though not pretending to any superior legal knowledge, his good sense, patience, impartiality and care, enabled him to perform his judicial functions very satisfactorily."

He is buried at Wistow, and in the church there is a mural tablet to his memory, with an inscription from the pen of his brother, Sir Henry Halford. His portrait, in his judge's robes, is in the great hall at Wistow.

IV. The very Reverend Peter Vaughan, educated, as were his brothers, at Rugby school, went thence to Merton College, Oxford, where he gained the Latin prize " Ars Chemica." He took his Arts degrees in due course and was elected a fellow of his College. In 1792 he became an assistant-master at Rugby school. He proceeded B.D. in 1806 and D.D. in 1810, and in that year was elected to the headship of his College—Warden of Merton. He was installed Dean of Chester 11th May, 1820, and died at Merton College, Oxford, 25th April, 1825.

V. William Welby Vaughan was born in 1772. He emigrated to Jamaica, and died there, unmarried, in 1803.

VI. The Right Hon. Sir Charles Vaughan was born at Leicester the 20th December, 1774. He, like his brother Henry, was bred to physic, but he diverted to the diplomatic line. He was educated at Rugby school, on leaving which, in 1791, he removed to Oxford and entered as a commoner at Merton College. He took the degree of B.A. in 1796, and then went to Edinburgh, where he spent two winter sessions in the study of medicine. He then returned to Oxford, and was elected a fellow of All Souls' College. In 1800 he proceeded Bachelor of Medicine, and

was elected one of the Radcliffe travelling fellows.
In conformity with the conditions of this endow-
ment he travelled—extensively and adventurously
—in Europe and Asia. In 1808, on the outbreak
of the insurrection in Spain against the usurpations
of Buonaparte, he repaired to Corunna. Thence
he went to Saragossa, where he made the intimate
acquaintance of Palafox, from whom he obtained
information of the celebrated siege of that place,
enabling him to publish an account of it in England, which contributed largely to increase the
sympathy of Englishmen with Spanish patriotism,
and which afterwards led to such great results.
From Saragossa he accompanied Palafox to the
encounter with the French armies in Arragon,
where, in a short time, the Spaniards were dis-
astrously defeated. Returning by way of Madrid
and thence to Corunna, he on his way conveyed
to Sir John Moore the first intimation of the
approach of an overwhelming force of the French
army, which created the necessity for an immediate retreat of the English. He embarked at
Corunna and returned for a time to England; but
shortly afterwards proceeded again to Spain,
accompanying Sir Henry Wellesley to Cadiz,
where he was present at the sittings of the Cortes.
Next he became Secretary of Legation to Sir

Henry Wellesley at Madrid.   He continued there after the conclusion of the war in the Peninsula, and during the absence of his chief performed, with great credit to himself, the duties of Minister there.

He next became Secretary to the Embassy at Paris, where his old friend, Sir Charles Stuart, was Ambassador; and from thence proceeded to Berne to represent British interests there, as Minister-Plenipotentiary in Switzerland.   He was afterwards for some years Minister to the United States of America, where he fully supported the honour of England, yet maintained at the same time great popularity with Americans by his amiable qualities and generous hospitality.   He returned to England in the beginning of 1831, was knighted in 1833, and was named a Privy Councillor in 1837.   His last appointment was that of Ambassador to Constantinople to replace Lord Ponsonby, who, owing to some misunderstanding, had intimated a desire for retirement; but matters having been arranged with him, Sir Charles Vaughan did not proceed to Turkey. He died, 15th June, 1849, and was buried at Kensal Green.   His portrait is in the great hall at Wistow.

VII. The Rev. Edward Thomas Vaughan,

the youngest of seven brothers, was also at Rugby school, from which he went, not to Oxford as had done four of his brothers, but to Cambridge—to Trinity College, where he took the two degrees in Arts, A.B. 1796, A.M. 1799, and was elected a fellow of that College. He received holy orders, and became vicar of St. Martin's, Leicester, and rector of the depopulated parish, Foston, in the same county. He died suddenly from disease of the heart at Foston, the 27th September, 1829, in the fifty-third year of his age. Mr. Vaughan's religious views were somewhat extreme. He was an uncompromising "evangelical," and his opinions were very strongly expressed, for he had a remarkable command of language. He was attentive and zealous in the discharge of his parochial duties and of great benevolence. His congregation and fellow-townsmen at Leicester were warmly attached to him, and this feeling was strongly attested at his funeral, during which the shops of the town were for the most part closed and business suspended. His parishioners of St. Martin's erected in that church a monument to his memory, on which is the following inscription, from the pen of Sir Henry Halford :

TO THE MEMORY OF

EDWARD THOMAS VAUGHAN, M.A.

A FAITHFUL AND ZEALOUS MINISTER OF THE GOSPEL
AND MORE THAN TWENTY-SEVEN YEARS VICAR OF THIS PARISH
WHO DIED SEPTEMBER 27TH, 1829, IN THE 53RD YEAR OF HIS AGE.
THIS MONUMENT WAS ERECTED
BY HIS AFFECTIONATE PARISHIONERS
TO RECORD THEIR ATTACHMENT AND GRATITUDE TO HIM
FOR HAVING TAUGHT THEM BY HIS DOCTRINE
AND LED THEM BY HIS EXAMPLE
THE WAY TO ETERNAL HAPPINESS
THROUGH JESUS CHRIST.

The above inscription would seem to most persons unexceptionable, but it failed to satisfy one friend of the deceased—Mr. Drummond, the banker and zealous Irvingite—who, in a letter to Sir Henry Halford, dated 19th May, 1830, subjected it to the following acute criticism :

" If you will not think me very presumptuous, and pardon me if you do, I should like to venture a remark or two upon your inscription. Your brother was as eminent in his line as you are in yours. And an inscription for him, difficult as such things are in all cases, is doubly so in his case. You would not think an inscription to Harvey perfect that did not notice his discovery respecting the blood ; nor that of Davy, which made no allusion to his chemical researches. In like manner the peculiar line of your brother's divinity, in which he reduced to system and consistency the loose declamations of Hooker, Charnock, Baxter and others, should, if possible, be noticed."

Mr. Drummond was a very old and intimate friend of Sir Henry Halford's, and one of his earliest patients in London. So far as I see this letter led to no alteration in Sir Henry's original draft of the inscription.

CHAPTER II

HENRY VAUGHAN'S EDUCATION, GENERAL AND
PROFESSIONAL

HENRY VAUGHAN, who subsequently became Sir Henry Halford, Bart., was the second but eldest surviving son of James Vaughan, M.D., of Leicester, by his wife Hester Smalley, and was born in Leicester on the 2nd October, 1766.

He was educated at Rugby school, and was admitted there in 1774, when but eight years of age, and earlier than had been intended by his father; who at that time went to Rugby, to place his eldest son, James, under the head-master, Mr. Stanley Burrough. They travelled from Leicester, a distance of about twenty miles, on horseback, and Henry, as a treat, was allowed to accompany them, with the intention that he should return with his father; but once at Rugby he entreated that he might remain and was permitted to do so. He was noted at Rugby for diligence and for the close attention with which he pursued his studies, and he there evinced that love of classical literature for which he was afterwards distinguished.

On leaving Rugby he proceeded to Oxford and was matriculated at Christ Church the 2nd of November, 1781, being then but fifteen years of age. He applied with zeal and success to all the subjects required for degrees in arts, especially to the Latin and Greek classics. He pondered over and mastered the beauties and subtleties of the several authors he read ; and came out, if not a deeply learned at the least a very elegant and graceful scholar. He availed himself, too, at Oxford of such aids as were there afforded for the study of subjects akin to the profession—that of medicine—for which he was destined. He attended the lectures of Dr. Martin Wall on chemistry, and those on clinical medicine by the same teacher at the Radcliffe Infirmary. His notes of the chemical course are full, and are a proof of the interest he took in the subject and of the thoroughness with which he studied it.

In due course he passed the exercises for his degree in arts, but he did not actually proceed to it till the 31st January, 1788. His M.A. dates the 17th June, 1788.

When about to leave Oxford he was addressed

by his elder brother, James Vaughan, then an undergraduate of Balliol, in the following lines, which, if not above the average of merit in juvenile poetry, are to the credit of both brothers as a testimony of affection.   They are, too, noteworthy as a prediction of the young student's professional success.

VERSES TO A BROTHER ON HIS LEAVING OXFORD TO STUDY PHYSICK IN EDINBURGH.

Ere yet, ingenuous youth, thy steps retreat
From Isis' banks, the Muse's favourite seat,
O let thy brother (and he boasts that name)
Breathe forth a verse, thy early virtues claim.
Let him in these few lines, this parting lay,
Some little token of his love betray,
Show that affection ever is the same,
That absence tends but to increase the flame;
And though thy worth a loftier strain requires,
A bard that's blessed with Pope's or Dryden's fires,
Haply thou may'st not with disdain refuse
The trifling product of an humbler Muse.
The time arrives when you must bid adieu
To Oxford's plains, and worthier scenes pursue;
When you must quit the present tedious plan,
And study Nature's laws in studying man.
No more in Christ Church walls shalt thou peruse
The lofty flights of Pindar's rapid Muse;
No more shall Virgil's captivating lay
E'er claim a portion of thy future day;
No more shalt thou consume the midnight oil
In studying Euclid with unwearied toil;
No more with fixed attention mark the page

Where Sylla burns with unrelenting rage,
Where Rome, well knowing her unhappy state,
Curses in vain the direful will of Fate.
Far worthier thoughts thy virtuous mind engage,
Thoughts that deserve thy care and suit thy age.
Lo ! where afar o'er yonder northern sky
Fair science rears her radiant head on high,
See in her hand a laurel crown she shows,
Waiting to decorate thy honoured brows.
Hark ! how she calls thee in melodious strain
To taste the pleasures of her learned train,
Bids thee to Oxford give a long adieu,
And dwell awhile amidst her chosen few.
Go then, fair youth, attend her grateful call,
There learn to raise the sinking e'er they fall,
Learn by unwearied diligence with ease
To check the rapid progress of disease ;
To quench the rage of fever's burning heat,
To replace health upon her long-lost seat,
To turn aside, with scientifick art,
Consumption's slow but never-erring dart.
Learn by thy healing influence to cheer
The downcast looks of sorrow and despair,
To pity those whom poverty hath made
Deserving objects of thy tender aid.
Thus shall thy days in endless bliss be past,
Each hour succeeding happier than the last,
While future ages shall thy praise proclaim,
And say, " This youth transcends his father's fame."

On quitting Oxford he went to Edinburgh, the
seat of a complete and excellent medical school.
In this he followed the example of our best
English physicians, who sought elsewhere the
medical instruction they could not obtain at

Oxford or Cambridge. Linacre, Caius and Harvey went to Padua; Mead and Sir George Baker to Leyden. Our future president selected Edinburgh, then at the zenith of its reputation, and as a school of medicine equal, in some points superior, to any other in Europe.

The full medical curriculum at Edinburgh comprised then, as now, three winter sessions, each of six months' duration—from November to the end of April. Henry Vaughan went through the entire course. He was there through the sessions of 1786–87, 1787–88 and 1788–89. Edinburgh was then at its best. Cullen was still living and lecturing, though in sequel to age failing somewhat. Anatomy was taught by the second and greatest of the Monros; Chemistry by Black; and the Institutes of Medicine by Gregory, the accomplished author of the "Conspectus Medicinæ Theoreticæ."

Henry Vaughan's attention was given especially to chemistry and anatomy. He attended two complete courses on the former subject, and three courses on the latter; and his notes of these, still at Wistow, are full, minute, and in their bearing essentially practical. He attended too, with diligence and great interest, the lectures of Dr. James Gregory, especially those on therapeutics, from which he learnt much.* He was assiduous, too, in his attendance upon the medical practice of the Royal Infirmary.

I dwell at length on the course of studies at Edinburgh because it was said very inaccurately, after Sir Henry Halford's death, by one of his surgical contemporaries,† that he was wanting in a scientific knowledge of his profession.   To this I shall refer more fully in a subsequent chapter.

In the intervals between the Edinburgh sessions he returned to Leicester and applied himself closely to the practical study of disease, at the bedside, under the able guidance of his father, an experienced and excellent physician, primarily and principally at the Leicester Infirmary, to which institution Dr. Vaughan was physician and of which he had been in great measure the founder.   He was, too, the almost constant companion and attendant on his father in his private practice, which was very extensive in Leicester and the surrounding country. Of these private cases the son took copious notes, which are still preserved at Wistow.   Among the patients to whom the younger Vaughan was thus

---

* The substance of these really remarkable lectures is to be seen in the second part—*Pars altera, in qua de Therapeia agitur*—of the " Conspectus Medicinæ Theoreticæ."

† Sir Benjamin Brodie.

introduced were many of the most distinguished
and well-known names in Leicestershire.

He proceeded Bachelor of Medicine at Oxford
on the 14th January, 1790, and then began to
practise on his own account.   He did so in the first
instance at Leicester in connection with but inde-
pendent of his father.   Among the persons who
then employed him are the names of several
families of consideration in Leicestershire : Earl
Ferrers, repeatedly, Lord Sherard, Sir Thomas
Apreece, Mrs. Bewicke, Miss Packe, &c., whose
good opinion and confidence he had probably
secured during his attendance on them with his
father

He took the degree of Doctor of Medicine at
Oxford 27th October, 1791, and about that time
planned to settle and establish himself as a physician at Scarborough.   This he proceeded to do
at the commencement of the next season there,
July, 1792.   He was probably attracted thither by
the circumstance that it was the favourite resort
of the best families of the Midland counties and
of many of his Leicestershire acquaintances.
His success at Scarborough was considerable, and
from his fee-book, now before me, I gather that in
the ten weeks he was there—from July 25th to
October 6th, 1792—he received in fees over one

hundred and thirty guineas.   Among his patients there were Lord Blayney, Lady E. Stewart, Lady Gavine, the Honourable Mrs. Kepple, and several other distinguished persons.

He entered into all the amusements of the place, and became known to and on friendly terms with most of the visitors there, by whom he was urged not to bury himself in a provincial town, and least of all in a summer watering-place, but try his fortune in London, and promising, should he do so, to exert all their influence for him there.

But he determined, before deciding, to consult Sir George Baker, the President of the College of Physicians and the acknowledged head of the medical profession in England.   In a visit to London some time before this he had become known to Sir George and had dined with him in Jermyn Street.   Among the guests on that occasion was Dr. Warton, the Provost of Eton, who in the course of the evening was seized with agonising pain in the loins due to the passage of a stone from the kidney.   He was attended to by Sir George and Dr. Vaughan; and the veteran physician was impressed by the ready assistance and nice discrimination of his young friend, and conceived a high opinion of his talents and of his prospects in the profession.

Sir George Baker, on being now consulted, told Dr. Vaughan that he stood little chance of earning a livelihood in the metropolis for five years, during which time he must support himself from other sources at the rate of about £300 a year. Nothing daunted, and doubtless confident in his own powers, he, with this intention (and the alternative in case of failure of returning to Leicester to take his father's position there), borrowed one thousand pounds of his patient and friend Lady Apreece, and on that capital commenced his career in London at the end of 1792. He resided in Queen Street, Mayfair, probably in apartments, and on the 20th February, 1793, was elected physician to the Middlesex Hospital. He was admitted a candidate of the College of Physicians the 25th March, 1793, and a fellow of that body the 14th April, 1794.

CHAPTER III

DR. HENRY VAUGHAN'S education, preliminary, general and professional, had been of the best kind—ample and complete in all its parts. By earnest study and close attention at the Infirmary of Edinburgh and under his father at Leicester he had already become a sound practical physician, to whom, as it would seem, nothing had been denied by nature and all that could be had been supplied by education. Thus fitted he entered on his medical career in London.

His Oxford connexions, his classical attainments and pleasing manners and the influence of his Leicestershire and Scarborough friends, soon introduced him into good society in London; and he secured for himself a position among the aristocracy by his marriage, on the 31st March, 1795, to the Honourable Elizabeth Barbara

St. John, the third daughter of John, eleventh Lord St. John of Bletsoe.

Dr. Vaughan's success would seem from the first to have been certain ; and Dr. Richard Warren, then the leading and most popular physician in London and a man of shrewd observation and sound judgment, predicted, on Dr. Vaughan's settling in London, that he would rise to the head of his profession.   His progress towards that position was rapid.   Before he had been a year in London, and while not yet twenty-seven years of age, he was sworn physician-extraordinary to the King.   There is no other instance in the annals of the Court, before or since this, of the appointment of so young a man to this or such an office.

Dr. Vaughan continued up to the time of his marriage to attend each summer at Scarborough for the three months of the season there.   In this he but followed the example of many young and promising London physicians.   His friend Dr. Warren had so attended at Tunbridge Wells, Sir Lucas Pepys at Brighton, and others at Bath, Harrogate and Buxton.

About the time of Dr. Vaughan's marriage he removed to Clarges Street, and remained there until 1802 when he went to Curzon Street—

No. 16—the fine and commodious house next to Wharncliffe House, where he lived the remainder of his life and in which he died.

By the year 1800 his private engagements had become so numerous that he was compelled to relinquish his office of physician to the Middlesex Hospital.

Several circumstances conspired about this time to add to his reputation and advance his interests. Upon St. Luke's day, 1800, he delivered the Harveian Oration to his colleagues, the fellows of the Royal College of Physicians. It was in choice Latin and in excellent taste throughout. His tribute to the memory of his friend Dr. Warren, then but recently dead, and his eulogy of the characters and services to the College and to the public of Dr. Heberden and Sir George Baker, both of whom were living but aged, were conceived in the best spirit and clothed in the choicest terms. The oration was generally admired and established his reputation as a scholar with the fellows of the College and with his friends and acquaintances outside it.

In the spring of 1806, Georgina, the beautiful Duchess of Devonshire, whose features are familiar to most persons from Gainsborough's unrivalled portrait, fell ill while dining at the

Marquis of Stafford's of a disorder, the seat and nature of which long eluded detection, although her Grace was attended by several of the most eminent physicians of the time. The illness began with severe pain in the back at about the level of the waist and to the right of the spine, on the subsidence of which shortly after there was a fever, irregular in its paroxysms and intermittent or remittent in type, the attacks of which terminated in copious sweats. Under this fever the body wasted and her Grace's strength rapidly declined. For the rest there was a weak and rapid pulse, and disorder of the stomach as evinced by frequent vomiting. The disease was thought to be aguish in character, and the bark was administered, but without any benefit.

After some days, when the anxiety about the Duchess had become extreme, Dr. Vaughan was added to the many physicians already in attendance. He had been in medical attendance on the Duke of Devonshire in the spring of 1804 and was so again after the death of the Duchess. He observed that in addition to the symptoms detailed above there was a yellowish tinge of the eyes and a deep brown hue of the skin during the febrile paroxysm, and that pain was produced by firm pressure in the region of the liver.

Dr. Vaughan concluded that the fever was a hectic, and its cause an abscess in the liver.   In this opinion he stood alone among his colleagues, but he adhered to it to the last.   The Duchess died, and on the examination of the body after death by Mr. subsequently Sir Everard Home, the only diseased conditions that could be detected were in the stomach and liver—gall stones, "tubercles," *and* what Dr. Vaughan had predicted, collections of matter or abscesses in the substance of that organ.

Attempts were made, especially by Mr. Home, to explain away these facts and to disparage Dr. Vaughan's diagnosis of the disease.   Under these circumstances Dr. Vaughan addressed to Lord John Townsend, an intimate friend of the Duke of Devonshire, the following letter :

"My Lord,

"As I have just reason to believe that the report which has been made of the appearances which presented themselves on examination of the body of the late Duchess of Devonshire is conveyed in technical terms so as to be scarcely intelligible to the family, I take the liberty of offering your Lordship a plain narrative, for the truth of which I pledge myself solemnly as a physician and a gentleman.

" On opening the head, the bloodvessels of the membranes investing the brain were all more turgid with blood than is usual, and a small portion of a colourless fluid was found effused between those membranes, and also into the cavities of the brain ; but not enough to be considered as a dropsy of the brain.

" The stomach was highly inflamed throughout the whole extent of its inner coat, and particularly about the lower orifice of it which leads into the intestines.

" The liver had a number of small tubercles on its surface, and the great lobe contained two of a larger size filled with matter. The small lobe was almost wholly occupied by another tubercle filled with matter. The bulk of the liver was rather more considerable than is common, and its substance more pulpy and of less firm texture than is usual.

" The gall bladder and ducts contained four gall stones, two of which were equal in magnitude each to a hazel nut, the others of a smaller size.

" A further examination of the other viscera was not thought necessary.

" How far these appearances confirm the opinion which I gave to my colleagues at our first consultation, and maintained at every subsequent one, and communicated frequently to your Lordship, previously to the melancholy termination of the Duchess's life, I leave it to your Lordship to judge. That opinion imported that I considered the fever not a primary disease, but as symptomatic of an imposthume in the liver.

"HENRY VAUGHAN."

This letter was communicated to the Duke of Devonshire, who replied to Lord John Townsend as follows :

"DEAR LORD JOHN,

"I am much obliged to you for your letter and write this to say that I am pretty well.

"With respect to what you say concerning Dr. Vaughan I have only to assure you that I am entirely and perfectly satisfied with his conduct, but it appears to me that declarations from me to that effect might seem to infer that it has been supposed that I was not so. I cannot imagine that there has been any such supposition, but if there has, it has been without the smallest degree of foundation.

"Yours sincerely,

"DEVONSHIRE."

In a correspondence which ensued between Dr. Vaughan, Sir Walter Farquhar, and Mr. Home, Dr. Vaughan gave expression to the following sensible remarks :

"I cannot reconcile it to myself to use terms of art when the fact may be explained in plain language."   And again, in another letter : " I object (and I objected at the time strenuously) to the use of *technical language* in the conveyance of that information to the family, which the Duke of Devonshire required, and more particularly to the statement of the principal fact of the case, in such terms of art as are intelligible only to the profession."

The facts of the Duchess of Devonshire's illness became widely known in the highest circles of society, and with the effect, as might be anticipated, of increasing Dr. Vaughan's reputation and adding largely to his professional engagements. Lady Halford told Dr. Francis Hawkins, that from the time of the Duchess of Devonshire's death, the door-bell in Curzon Street was rarely still, and that thenceforth there was never any want of patients.

One of the many patients attracted to Dr. Vaughan, in consequence of the Duchess of Devonshire's case, was the statesman, Charles James Fox.   He was one of her Grace's most attached friends, and had been an anxious observer of all that occurred during the course of her illness.   Mr. Fox's health had then been failing for some months, and continued to do so in marked degree through the whole month of March, 1806, when his friends were convinced that he was fast breaking.   At this time he consulted Dr. Vaughan, who urged the necessity of care, attention and quiet, and under his treatment there was, for a time, a marked improvement in Mr. Fox's condition.   In June, however, the symptoms returned with redoubled violence, and by the end of that month decided signs of dropsy appeared.   Dr. Vaughan was now again called in ; and, as we are told by Lord Holland, was allowed to examine Mr. Fox more minutely than he had hitherto permitted him or any other physician to do. Though neither impatient nor desponding in sickness, Mr. Fox had little confidence in medical skill, and less curiosity even on subjects connected with the health and management of the human body than on any other.   Medicines now failed to relieve, and tapping was had recourse to once and again.   But the disease ran its usual course, and ended fatally the 13th September, 1806.

The following letter from Lord Holland to Dr. Vaughan is not dated, but must have been written soon after Dr. Vaughan resumed his attendance and treatment—*i.e.*, about June 26th, 1806.

" DEAR SIR,

" I found my uncle much satisfied with his conversation with you, and highly pleased with

the clearness with which you explained to him
your views of his case. As, therefore, he is so
much disposed to talk openly to you without
reserve, I hope you have fixed some hour to be
there to-morrow, and if you have, I will thank
you to let me know when it is, as I wish to meet
you there.   " Yours,

                              " HOLLAND."

Among Dr. Vaughan's early medical friends in
London, those to whom as a junior physician he
was accustomed to look up, and to consult when
consultation was needed, were in the first place
Sir George Baker and Dr. Warren, then Dr.
Revell Reynolds and Sir Walter Farquhar, and
later, Dr. Matthew Baillie. Of Dr. Warren and
Dr. Baillie I have spoken enough elsewhere in this
volume.

Sir George Baker was a profound and elegant
scholar, the soundness of whose judgment was
acknowledged by all. To him the whole medical
world looked up with respect, and in the treatment of any disease in the least degree unusual, if
it was desired to know all that had ever been said
or written on the subject, from the most remote
antiquity down to the case in question, a consultation was proposed with Sir George Baker. From
his erudition everything was expected. He was

particularly kind to the rising members of his profession, whom he encouraged and informed with
great condescension and apparent interest;* as he
had done in an especial manner Dr. Vaughan,
when consulted by him, as to the chances of his
success as a physician in the metropolis. Sir
George Baker and Dr. Warren were the two
senior physicians to whom Dr. Vaughan was
accustomed to look for consultation and aid in
the earliest years of his practice in London.

Dr. Reynolds was an able physician, and on the
death of Dr. Warren succeeded to one of the best
medical practices in the metropolis. We are told
by his contemporaries that he was singularly
happy in the selection and combination of his
remedies. "There was something introduced for
every symptom or even inconvenience, yet the
whole harmonised and had immediate reference to
the principal complaint." I have before me notes
of some of Dr. Vaughan's consultations with Dr.
Reynolds, and of hints derived from him, on the
actions and uses of drugs and the treatment of
diseases. I have little doubt that some part
at least of Sir Henry Halford's characteristics
in practice and acknowledged excellence in the

* *The Gold-headed Cane*, edited by William Munk, M.D.
8vo. London, 1884, p. 138.

art of prescribing, were derived from Dr. Reynolds.

Sir Walter Farquhar was a physician of large experience and sound judgment in physic. He was a warm and steady friend, ever ready to forward merit where he found it, and he did so in the instance of Dr. Vaughan, especially in the case of the Duchess of Devonshire and in the controversy that ensued upon it, siding with him at this, a very critical moment in his medical history.

Dr. Vaughan's business, even before his attendance on the Duchess of Devonshire, was already very large, and his professional income considerable. In the year 1805 it had amounted to more than seven thousand seven hundred pounds, and there were few families of station or note in England, by one or more members of which he had not been consulted. His list of patients previous to this, comprises a large number of persons of rank, and many eminent in politics and in all departments of public life.

Among them were their Royal Highnesses the Duke and Duchess of Gloucester, the Duke of Kent, the Duke of Cumberland and the Duke of York. Mr. Wilberforce was among the early and most constant of his patients. The names also occur, and most of them repeatedly, of Mr. Henry Thornton, Mr. George Tierney, Mr. Whitbread, Mr. Windham, and Mr. Baring ; of Lord Carlisle, Lord Essex, Mr. Pusey, the Hon. Spencer Perceval, Lord and Lady Holland, the Earl of Chatham, Lady Hester Stanhope, and Mr. Pitt ; the Duke and Duchess of Bedford, Lord Grey, General Granville, Lord Carnarvon, Lord Thurlow, Mr. Canning, Earl Grosvenor, Mr. Charles Greville, Sir James Graham, Lord Granville, Warren Hastings, the Dukes of Devonshire, of Grafton, and of Hamilton, the Marquis of Lansdowne and the Earl of Westmoreland ; and of the Church, the primates, Dr. Markham of York, and Dr. Moore and Dr. Manners Sutton of Canterbury, the bishops of St. Asaph, Cork, Lichfield, Winchester, Bristol, St. David's, and Durham. These are but a few of the distinguished persons who had then consulted him.

"No physician," it has been truly said, "acquires a high reputation *and retains* an extensive practice who is really unworthy of it. The public are on the whole pretty good judges in a matter in which they are so much interested, and if by any accident they have been led to give their confidence to a wrong person, they are seldom long in discovering and correcting their mistake."

Dr. Vaughan's progress to the highest position in the medical profession was so rapid yet withal so steady as to prove that his reputation increased as his skill was more and more subjected to the tests supplied by an increasing demand for it. He attained rapidly, and without perceptible extraneous aid, the largest physician's practice and the most extensive reputation, and he maintained a supremacy in both for the longest period known in this country.

It may be added that Dr. Vaughan's list of patients, even at the period of which I am now writing, had comprised not only persons of high quality, but a greater number of leading characters in the State—of persons having a free choice of their physician, and whose power of judgment in the selection cannot be questioned—than perhaps ever before or since had fallen to the lot of any English physician.

The following account of the professional income made by Dr. Vaughan in each year, from 1792, when he settled in London, to 1809, when he was called in to attend the Princess Amelia at Windsor, and was admitted into close relations with the Court, may have an interest as part of the social history of that time.

His professional receipts in his

				£		
1st	year,	1792,	were	£220	0	0
2nd	„	1793	„	164	0	0
3rd	„	1794	„	327	0	0
4th	„	1795	„	401	0	0
5th	„	1796	„	399	0	0
6th	„	1797	„	511	0	0
7th	„	1798	„	905	0	0
8th	„	1799	„	1403	0	0
9th	„	1800	„	2153	0	0
10th	„	1801	„	3214	0	0
11th	„	1802	„	5081	0	0
12th	„	1803	„	5947	0	0
13th	„	1804	„	7632	0	0
14th	„	1805	„	7727	0	0
15th	„	1806	„	7909	0	0
16th	„	1807	„	9434	0	0
17th	„	1808	„	8942	0	0
18th	„	1809	„	9850	0	0

In the year last named—1809—Dr. Vaughan, under circumstances to be explained in the next chapter, became Sir Henry Halford, Bart., and will be so designated in the following pages.

After 1809 he was much in attendance on the Royal Family at Windsor, and on the Prince of Wales at Carlton House. There are no documents at hand showing the exact amount of his professional income after 1809. On one or two occasions it is known to have amounted to £12,000 in the year; as, for instance, in 1824, when he received the following letter:

"WINDSOR CASTLE, 28th *March*, 1824.

" DEAR SIR HENRY,

"I am honoured with the commands of the King to convey to you his Majesty's very kind regards and to transmit the sum of two thousand pounds as an acknowledgment for your professional attendance from time to time on his Majesty.

"I am further commanded to express to you how sensibly his Majesty feels your zealous, dutiful and affectionate attention on all occasions.

"I have the honour to be, dear Sir Henry,

"Your sincere and faithful servant,

"W. KNIGHTON,

"*Privy Purse.*

"Sir HENRY HALFORD, Bart."

But with such exceptions as these, Sir Henry's professional income is known to have been steadily over £10,000 for a long series of years; indeed, until a few years before his death and up to 1837, when William IV. died and his attendance on the Court terminated.

It may not perhaps be out of place here to say a few words on the professional earnings of English, and especially of London, physicians. The amount of revenue sometimes enters into the computation of a medical character, and I may be pardoned if I dwell upon it here. But it must be observed first, that the average income of physicians is much less than it is thought by the public to be, and that the enormous amounts said to have been made by some physicians may be summarily dismissed as fabulous, for there are neither hours enough in the day nor days enough in the year in which, with the fees that have been current among us, such large amounts could have been realised. And further, it must be remembered that the large incomes I am about to mention are exceptional—they were made by the most popular of the faculty only—by one or two it may be, at one and the same time of the favourite and foremost of the London physicians.

The great reputation which Dr. Radcliffe had made at Oxford preceded him to London, and secured him from the first a very large professional income. It has been always understood that from an early period he made on an average twenty guineas a day, or more than seven thousand a year; which amount was soon increased, though to what extent is not known, and continued much the same to the death of William III. Dr. Mead, the protégé of Radcliffe and his successor in public favour, had a professional income of from five to six thousand guineas for many successive years, and in one year he received as much as seven thousand.

The elder Dr. Warren, who died in 1797, one of
the most popular of men and the favourite physician of his time, realised for some years nine
thousand a year and bequeathed to his family
one hundred and fifty thousand pounds.   Dr.
Matthew Baillie's income for many years ranged
from nine to ten thousand, and Sir Henry
Halford's professional income from the time when
he was called into attendance on the Prince
Regent to the death of William IV., when his
immediate attendance on the Court terminated, is
known to have generally exceeded ten thousand
guineas, and on one or two occasions, as above
stated, it amounted to twelve thousand a year.
This is probably a larger professional income than
at that time had ever been made for a long series
of years—it was more than a quarter of a century—
by any English physician.   Dr. Chambers, who
succeeded to the position in public estimation and
professional employment that had been so long
occupied by Sir Henry Halford, had a professional income ranging for some years between
seven and nine thousand a year, but he never
exceeded, it is believed, the larger amount.

A few words on fees for long journeys and
special services will conclude what remains to be
said on the emoluments and *honoraria* of physi-

cians.   Radcliffe, for going to Namur in 1695 to attend on Lord Albemarle, with whom he remained a week, received from William III. twelve hundred pounds, and from Lord Albemarle himself four hundred guineas and a diamond ring. Dr. Dimsdale, the founder of a well-known banking house in the City, who had achieved a high reputation for his management of smallpox and his method of inoculating that disease, was called by the Empress Catherine of Russia to St. Petersburg in 1768 ; and for his successful inoculation of the Empress herself and of her son the Grand Duke, was rewarded with the rank of Baron of the Empire, Councillor of State and physician to the Empress, with a pension of five hundred pounds per annum, and a present in money of twelve thousand pounds.   Dr. Granville, for a journey to St. Petersburg in the first half of the present century, received one thousand pounds and his travelling expenses going and returning ; and I know that a well-known and popular physician of the present day received on two occasions a thousand guineas for going to Pau ; and further, that the same physician had a fee of fifteen hundred guineas for going to Pitlochry and remaining there with his patient for a week.

For long journeys and special services such as

those above mentioned, there is no established or fixed rate of remuneration. But it is not so with shorter journeys or those within our own shores. In posting and coaching times, professional journeys into the country were remunerated at the rate of a guinea a mile, the distance being reckoned from the physician's house to the abode of the patient, and no account being taken of the journey back. But this rate of remuneration was thought by some grateful patients to be inadequate, and larger fees were pressed upon the physician. It was often so in the case of Sir Henry Halford. Thus, I find the note of a fee of one hundred guineas for a visit to Woburn Abbey, a distance of some fifty miles from London, and one of five hundred guineas from the Duke of Cleveland for a hasty visit to Newton House, Bedale, in Yorkshire, a distance of less than two hundred and thirty miles from the metropolis.

When railroads had become general throughout the country, it was felt by some of the leading physicians and surgeons of the metropolis, that an easier, less tedious and less expensive mode of travelling ought in fairness to the public, to be met by some reduction in the rate of remuneration ; and after a full consideration of all the circumstances it was concluded, in sequel to a conference

between Dr. Paris and Sir Benjamin Brodie, on
the part respectively of the College of Physicians
and of the College of Surgeons, that a reduction
of one-third would be fair to all parties, and meet
all the requirements of the case; and thus, that a
physician's journey of three hundred miles would
imply a fee of two hundred guineas, in the place
of three hundred as it had previously done.

CHAPTER IV

UNDER the will of Sir Charles Halford, the last baronet of the first creation, who died in 1780, Dr. Henry Vaughan, as the eldest surviving son of James Vaughan, M.D., of Leicester, was to succeed to the Halford estate of Wistow after the death of Sir Charles' widow. She married in July 1793 as her second husband Basil, sixth earl of Denbigh, outlived him, and survived until 1814.

In the year 1809, Dr. Henry Vaughan changed his name by Act of Parliament to that of Halford, and somewhat later—on the 27th September, 1809—as a mark of royal favour, was created a baronet.

In the December following, Sir Henry Halford was called with Dr. Baillie into medical attendance on the Princess Amelia at Windsor, and they together continued to attend her Royal Highness until her death. Very shortly after that event Sir Henry Halford was consulted about George III., and with Dr. Baillie and other physicians continued to attend the King for ten years, until his death in 1820. In the autumn of 1810 the Prince of Wales appointed Sir Henry one of his physicians in ordinary, and secured for him in 1812 the appointment of physician in ordinary to the King. But of Sir Henry Halford's services to the several members of the Royal Family further particulars will be given in a subsequent chapter.

The Government at this time, through Lord Palmerston, consulted Sir Henry Halford as to the honorarium that ought to be made to Dr. (afterwards Sir) Gilbert Blane for his expedition to Walcheren, for the purpose of reporting on the state of the army there.

It may be thought that the president of the College of Physicians—and Sir Henry Halford did not become so till ten years later—was the proper person to apply to for advice under these circumstances. But Sir Lucas Pepys, then the president, was not in favour with the authorities, general or military. He was, and had been for many years, physician-general to the army and president of the Army Medical Board, which had not worked satisfactorily or smoothly under his guidance. Sir Lucas was ordered as physician-general to proceed to Walcheren to report on the exceptional sickness and mortality of the army there. But in an evil hour he declined to go, assigning as his reason that he was not acquainted with the diseases of soldiers in camp or in quarters.* Unfortunately neither of the other two members of the Board volunteered their services, and under these circumstances, Dr. Blane was selected and went. Lord Palmerston's letter was as follows :

"WAR OFFICE, *February* 13, 1810.

" Lord Palmerston presents his compliments to Sir Henry Halford, and has many apologies to make to him for the liberty he is about to take ; but finding a considerable difficulty in forming any opinion as to the amount of the sum which it would be proper for him to recommend to the Treasury to be offered to Dr. Blane as a remuneration for his trouble in undertaking an expedition to Walcheren, for the purpose of reporting upon the state of Lord Chatham's army, Lord Palmerston conceives that Sir Henry Halford may from

* "The Autobiography and Services of Sir James McGrigor, Bart., late Director of the Army Medical Department." London, 1861, p. 242.

his professional knowledge be enabled to assist him by some suggestion upon this subject.

"Lord Palmerston is fully aware of the delicacy attaching to matters of this sort, and would not have taken the liberty of addressing Sir Henry on this occasion had he not reason to believe that it was consistent with the wishes of Dr. Blane himself that he should do so.   Lord P. feels it unnecessary to add that he conceives this to be a strictly confidential communication."

Sir Henry replied as follows :

"My Lord,

"It is difficult to appreciate satisfactorily Dr. Blane's services under the circumstances which your Lordship states ; but as you do me the honour to write to me confidentially, I will tell you what I think without reserve.

"I should suppose that £1500 would be a liberal remuneration, without risk of being thought a prodigal one.   It is not material to the case how much or how little inconvenience the Doctor might sustain in his private affairs by his absence at Walcheren ; nor do I allow it to bias my judgment that he knew he was to encounter some personal hazard by his attendance on the sick there ; a physician should never consider that, but the occasion was an extraordinary one. He obeyed the directions of the Commander-in-Chief instantly, and *his patient was an army.*

"In this point of view I really think Dr. Blane's reward should be one of magnitude, though I admit that the public purse should be opened on all occasions with more caution and reserve than that of an individual, and particularly at this time.

"I am, my Lord,

"Your faithful servant,

"HENRY HALFORD."

Sir Henry Halford had been a warm advocate of Vaccination from its introduction by Dr. Jenner in 1798, and he continued so up to his death. But in May 1811 a case occurred in his own practice, which cast much doubt on the protective power of vaccination against smallpox, and was the subject of much anxious thought and comment at the time. Alleged cases of smallpox after vaccination had been reported before, but none in which Dr. Jenner himself had been the operator. For thirteen years Jenner had been carrying on vaccination on a very extended scale, and of the many thousands who had been subsequently exposed to the influence of smallpox, not one was known to have been affected by that disease.

But on the 26th May, 1811, the Hon. Robert Grosvenor, a son of Earl Grosvenor, was seized with symptoms which denote the approach of a very

violent disease.   In four days he became delirious
and an eruption appeared upon the face.   At that
time the existence of smallpox was not suspected,
either by Sir Henry Halford or Sir Walter Farquhar, who were in attendance, because their
patient had been vaccinated by Dr. Jenner some
ten years before.   In the course of the following
day, however, the eruption increased immensely,
and some of the worst symptoms of a confluent
and malignant smallpox showed themselves.
The two physicians in making their report of the
case, observed that they entertained a most unfavourable opinion of the issue of the malady,
having never seen an instance of recovery under
so heavy an eruption.   It seemed, however, to use
their own words in a later report, "that the latter
stages of the disease were passed through more
rapidly in this case than usual ; and it may be a
question whether this extraordinary circumstance,
as well as the ultimate recovery of Master Grosvenor was not influenced by the previous vaccination."   There can be no doubt now that it was so.
The disease went through its course in a shorter
period than usual, without any secondary fever
and left scarcely any marks.

Dr. Jenner, who happened to be in London, and
saw the case, at once admitted the failure and ex-

plained it.   He had vaccinated this young gentleman in a puny state of health when about a month
old.   Lady Grosvenor was timid and prevailed
on Dr. Jenner to deviate from his usual mode of
practice, and to make one puncture only ; and the
pustule it excited was unfortunately deranged in
its progress by being rubbed by the nurse.*

It should be added that the other children of
the Earl, who had been vaccinated in 1801, were
exposed to the contagion of smallpox under which
their brother was suffering and were also inoculated
for the smallpox, but without any effect.

This disastrous occurrence in Lord Grosvenor's
family and some other like cases which occurred
about this time, induced the Board of the National
Vaccine Establishment to issue a special report ;
a measure which was rendered necessary in consequence of the alarm and consternation in the
minds of those whose children had been vaccinated.   Notwithstanding this and some similar
cases, Sir Henry Halford's estimate of vaccination
as a *generally* preventive and modifying influence
against smallpox continued high.   And so highly,
years after this, did he appreciate vaccination and
the merits of Jenner in relation to it, that in
the arrangement of the royal household at the

* Baron's " Life of Jenner," vol. ii. pp. 156 and 267.

accession of George IV. he was instrumental in obtaining for Dr. Jenner the appointment of physician-extraordinary to the king.

On Sir Henry's appointment to the presidency of the College of Physicians, he became ex-officio president of the National Vaccine Establishment, in which institution was vested the direction of all matters relating to vaccination, and the supply of the lymph necessary to that operation; and he was a diligent attendant at the meetings of the board. The information communicated to the board of the establishment from parts domestic and foreign, was of the most interesting and satisfactory character, and confirmed all the conclusions to which he had previously reached, of the safety, efficacy, and manifold advantages of vaccination, *when practised with all the care and all the precautions so strongly enforced by Dr. Jenner.*

In the spring of 1813 an event of some historical interest occurred, in which Sir Henry Halford was called upon to take a prominent part. This was the opening of the coffin of Charles I. with a view to its identification.

It was not known precisely where in St. George's Chapel at Windsor the body of Charles I. had been interred. Mr. Herbert, who had been

a groom of the bedchamber and a faithful companion of the king from the time he left the Isle
of Wight until his death, was employed to convey
the body of the king to Windsor, and to fix
upon a proper place for his interment there, and
was an eye-witness to that interment, states distinctly that it was in the vault of Henry VIII.
But Lord Clarendon in his history of the Rebellion
tells us, that some years afterwards a most careful search was made for the body by several
people, amongst whom were some of those noble
persons whose faithful attachment had led them
to pay their last tribute of respect to their unfor-
tunate master by attending his body to the grave.
Yet such had been the injury done to the chapel,
such were the mutilations it had undergone,
during the period of the usurpation, that no
marks were left by which the *exact* place of burial
of the king could be ascertained.   But the fact is,
King Charles I. was buried in the vault of King
Henry VIII., situated precisely where Mr. Herbert has described it ; and an accident has served
to elucidate a point in history, which the great
authority of Lord Clarendon had involved in some
obscurity.

On completing the mausoleum which George
III. built in the tomb house, as it is called, it was

necessary to form a passage to it from under the choir of St. George's Chapel. In constructing this passage an aperture was made accidentally in one of the walls of the vault of King Henry VIII. through which the workmen were enabled to see not only the two coffins which were supposed to contain the bodies of King Henry VIII. and Queen Jane Seymour, but a third also, covered with a black velvet pall, which from Mr. Herbert's narrative, might fairly be presumed to hold the remains of King Charles I.

On representing the circumstance to the Prince Regent, his Royal Highness perceived at once, that a doubtful point in history might be cleared up by opening this vault ; and accordingly his Royal Highness ordered an examination to be made on the first convenient opportunity. This was done on the first of April 1813, the day after the funeral of the Duchess of Brunswick, in the presence of his Royal Highness himself, who guaranteed thereby the most respectful care and attention to the remains of the dead, during the inquiry. His Royal Highness was accompanied by H.R.H. the Duke of Cumberland, Count Munster, the dean of Windsor, Benjamin Charles Stevenson, Esq., and Sir Henry Halford.

On removing the pall, a plain leaden coffin, with no appearance of ever having been encased in wood, and bearing an inscription :

KING CHARLES—1648,

in large legible characters, on a scroll of lead encircling it, immediately presented itself to the view. A square opening was then made in the upper part of the lid of such dimensions as to admit a clear insight into its contents. These were an internal wooden coffin very much decayed, and the body carefully wrapped in cere-cloth, into the folds of which a quantity of unctuous or greasy matter mixed with resin, as it seemed, had been melted, so as to exclude as effectually as possible the external air. The coffin was completely full, and from the tenacity of the cere-cloth, great difficulty was experienced in detaching it success-fully from the parts which it enveloped. Wherever the unctuous matter had insinuated itself, the separation of the cere-cloth was easy ; and when it came off a correct impression of the features to which it had been applied was observed in the unctuous substance. At length the whole face was disengaged from its covering. The com-plexion of the skin of it was dark and discoloured. The forehead and temples had lost little or nothing of their muscular substance; the cartilage of the nose was gone; but the left eye in the first moment of exposure was open and full, though it vanished almost immediately : and the pointed beard, so characteristic of the period of the reign of King Charles, was perfect. The shape of the face was a long oval ; many of the teeth remained ; and the left ear, in consequence of the interposition of the unctuous matter between it and the cere-cloth, was found entire.

It was difficult, at the moment, to withhold a declaration, that, notwithstanding its disfigure-ment, the countenance did bear a strong re-semblance to the coins, the busts, and especially to the pictures of King Charles I. by Vandyke, by which it had been made familiar to us. It is true that the minds of the spectators of this interesting sight were well prepared to receive this impression, but it is also certain that such a facility of belief had been occasioned by the sim-plicity and truth of Mr. Herbert's narrative, every part of which had been confirmed by the investi-gation so far as it had advanced : and it will not be denied that the shape of the face, the forehead, an eye, and the beard, are the most important features by which resemblance is determined.

When the head had been entirely disengaged

from the attachments which confined it, it was found to be loose, and without any difficulty was taken up and held to view. It was quite wet, and gave a greenish red tinge to paper and to linen which touched it. The back part of the scalp was entirely perfect and had a remarkably fresh appearance; the pores of the skin being more distinct, as they usually are when soaked in moisture; and the tendons and ligaments of the neck were of considerable substance and firmness. The hair was thick at the back part of the head, and, in appearance, nearly black. A portion of it since cleaned and dried is of a beautiful dark brown colour. That of the beard was a redder brown. On the back part of the head it was more than an inch in length, and had probably been cut so short for the convenience of the executioner; or perhaps by the piety of friends soon after death, in order to furnish memorials of the unhappy king.

On holding up the head to examine the place of separation from the body, the muscles of the neck had evidently retracted themselves considerably; and the fourth cervical vertebra was found to be cut through its substance transversely, leaving the surface of the divided portions perfectly smooth and even, an appearance which could have been produced only by a heavy blow, inflicted with a very sharp instrument, and which furnished the last proof wanting to identify King Charles the First.

After this examination of the head, which served every purpose in view, and without examining the body below the neck, it was immediately restored to its situation, the coffin was soldered up again, and the vault closed.

Neither of the other coffins had any inscription upon them.   The larger one, supposed on good grounds to contain the remains of King Henry VIII., measured six feet ten inches in length, and had been enclosed in an elm one of two inches in thickness; but this was decayed and lay in small fragments near it.   The leaden coffin appeared to have been beaten in by violence about the middle, and a considerable opening in that part of it exposed a mere skeleton of the king.   Some beard remained upon the chin, but there was nothing to discriminate the personage contained in it.

The smaller coffin, understood to be that of Queen Jane Seymour, was not touched; mere curiosity not being considered by the Prince Regent as a sufficient motive for disturbing these remains.

On examining the vault with some attention, it

was found that the wall at the west end had, at some period or other, been partly pulled down and repaired again, not by regular masonry, but by fragments of stones and bricks, put rudely and hastily together without cement.

From Lord Clarendon's account, as well as from Mr. Herbert's narrative of the interment of King Charles, it is to be inferred that the ceremony was a very hasty one, performed in the presence of the governor, who had refused to allow the service according to the Book of Common Prayer to be used on the occasion ; and had, probably, scarcely permitted the time necessary for a decent deposit of the body. It is not unlikely therefore that the coffin of King Henry VIII. had been injured by a precipitate introduction of the coffin of King Charles ; and that the governor was not under the influence of feelings, in those times, that gave him any concern about royal remains or the vault which contained them.

When the manuscript containing the above account was read to the Prince Regent, by whose command it had been drawn up by Sir Henry Halford, his Royal Highness was pleased to desire that he might authenticate it, which he did immediately previous to its being deposited in the

British Museum. It is from the published copy of it, in Sir Henry Halford's " Essays and Orations," that the above account, slightly abridged, has been transcribed.

It was found after the coffin of King Charles had been soldered up, that the portion of the vertebra which had been cut through, had separated from the neck, and fallen aside unnoticed, and so had escaped restoration to the coffin. It was not deemed necessary by the Prince Regent that the coffin should be again opened to replace the bone, which his Royal Highness then, with several kind expressions, presented to Sir Henry Halford as a memorial of the poor king himself, and as a mark of his own esteem for him.

Sir Henry, who valued the relic very highly, had a case carved of lignum vitæ lined with gold and a fitting Latin inscription inside the lid, in which he placed it, and in which it was scrupulously kept as long as it remained in the Halford family. It was shown at times to persons curious about it, and its existence in Sir Henry's possession thus became known and was somewhat severely commented on. The present representative of the family, Sir Henry St. John Halford, to whom it had descended, not feeling quite at ease in its possession and custody, sought an interview with H.R.H. the Prince of Wales and restored it to his hands. His Royal Highness has, it is understood, returned it to the vault and deposited it in its case on the coffin of Charles I., where it now reposes.

Lady Denbigh* died at Brighton, 2nd October, 1814, when Sir Henry Halford succeeded to the Halford estate of Wistow in Leicestershire. Wistow came into the possession of the Halfords in 1603. Richard Halford of Wistow, famed for his loyalty, was high sheriff of Leicestershire, 19 James I.; and in 1640 was committed to the Tower by the Parliamentarians, but was soon liberated. On the 28th December, 1641 he was created a baronet by Charles I. He was so remarkable for his loyalty that the king, when in Leicestershire, made Wistow his chief abode; where Sir Richard Halford not only entertained his sovereign, but supplied him with considerable sums of money. The king on his way into Leicestershire slept at Wistow, a few days before the battle of Naseby. The room in which he did so is still in use and is but little altered. The king, defeated at Naseby, fled for Leicester, and on his way changed horses at Wistow, but was so

* *Vide* p. 46.

closely pursued, he did not dare stay to have his saddle changed. The king's saddle and that of Prince Rupert, who accompanied him, were left at Wistow, and are to be seen in good preservation in a glass case in the inner hall. The king left his sword also at Wistow, but that was by Sir Henry Halford presented to and graciously accepted by George IV. It was placed in St. George's Hall, Windsor, where it probably now is.

When Sir Henry Halford succeeded to the estate in 1814, the rent roll of the property was £3200 a year. It comprised, as a part only of the estate, the entire parish of Wistow, which it may be stated contained but two houses, the Hall and one other. Sir Henry often declared to his friends that he was a rich man before he came into Wistow, but had been a poor man ever after. And this seems to have been the fact. The Hall and all the buildings on the estate had been sadly neglected and were greatly dilapidated when Sir Henry obtained possession of them. His first care was to repair and restore them, but many years elapsed ere this was accomplished and more than the annual proceeds of the estate were needed to do it. This had to be supplied from his professional income.

He made considerable alterations and additions to the Hall and rendered it comfortable and convenient in all its internal arrangements. He reconstructed the dining-room, and made the present suite of drawing-rooms. The grounds around the house were much improved. He planted largely and judiciously, made pleasant walks in the wood and shrubberies, excavated a deep lake of two acres and a half, where there was none before, and erected a belvidere on a raised spot, at a short distance from the Hall. It was not for two years after Sir Henry came into possession that the Hall was fitted to receive him.

From an early period of his married life, Sir Henry had had a house out of town, but in its neighbourhood, in what was then the country— for his wife and children, to which he himself frequently resorted. In 1801 it was at Hayes in Middlesex, in 1802 at Barnes, in the following year at Fulham, and in 1805 at Barnes again. This last was a house of some size and pretensions, and he seems to have kept it on until he succeeded to Wistow and it was fitted to receive him. From that time—1816—it was his custom to pass the greater part of three months of the year, July, August and September, at Wistow; and he greatly valued this " his retirement in the summer."

From a letter of Sir Henry Halford's, dated March, 1823, it appears that in 1814 when he succeeded to Wistow the rent roll of the property was £3200 a year, and that in 1823 it was nominally £4200, but times were then bad and a return was being made to the tenants. In the interval, however, he had spent £12,000 in adding to the property, £23,500 in paying off mortgages, and he had laid out £30,000 on the hall, farms, parsonage and church. It may be added that between 1823 and 1844 he added still more to the Wistow estate.

At Wistow, Sir Henry Halford was the country gentleman, and maintained much state. He had four horses and postillions to his carriage, entertained largely, and did so handsomely. The house was generally full of company, for he received not only his Leicestershire friends but many more from afar, from London and elsewhere; among whom were many of the highest and most distinguished persons of the time. In 1840 he had the honour of receiving H.R.H. the Duke of Cambridge; and the Duke of Rutland in a letter to Sir Henry Halford, dated 3rd September, 1840, writes : " The Duke of Cambridge was delighted with Wistow and with the hospitality he experienced there. I had a letter from him while there expressing himself in strong terms on the subject."

Sir Henry Halford's attendance on George III. continued through the decade from 1810 to 1820. For the first twelve or eighteen months of it his attendance was close and frequent. At least half of the year 1811 was spent by him at Windsor, much to the derangement and detriment of his practice in town. But great hopes were then entertained of the king's recovery, and it was felt by Sir Henry and his especial colleague Dr. Baillie that no effort of theirs should be wanting to bring about so desirable an event. When, however, all thoughts of the king's recovery were given up, an attendance once only in the week by each physician was deemed sufficient, and Sir Henry was enabled to resume his usual professional routine in London.

During this decade Sir Henry was increasing his reputation and business, and strengthening his position at Court and amongst the highest and most distinguished of the land.

CHAPTER V

THE year 1820 was an eventful one in the life of Sir Henry Halford. In January, George III. died after an illness of ten years ; and Sir Henry's great patron, the Prince Regent, succeeded as George IV. From that time Sir Henry occupied a prominent and really important position about the King, and with all the members of the Royal Family.

In September, 1820, Sir Henry was elected president of the Royal College of Physicians, and as such became the recognised head of the medical profession in England, a position he continued to occupy worthily for nearly a quarter of a century. Of his services to the College of Physicians I shall speak at large in a subsequent chapter. Suffice it here to say, that he infused into the College a spirit and an energy which it had not possessed for more than a century, and the effects of which are felt and visible even to the present day.

Sir Henry Halford on becoming president of the College of Physicians became ex-officio a trustee of the British Museum, in the management of which institution he soon became warmly interested. He was a trustee when George IV. presented to the nation the fine library that had been collected by his father George III. and the keeping of which he entrusted to the British Museum. Sir Henry was one of several scholars who suggested inscriptions to be placed in the hall commemorative of the gift and of the donor. His was as follows:

HANC OMNIGENÆ SUPELLECTILIS LITERARIÆ COPIAM

A GEORGIO TERTIO BRITANNIARUM REGE

SUMMÂ CURÂ ET SUMPTU VERÈ REGIO

COMPARATAM;

GEORGIUS REX, FILIUS

PATERNÆ BENIGNITATIS ERGA LITERATOS MEMOR,

IPSE ARTIUM LIBERALIUM PATRONUS EXIMIUS

ANNO REGNI SUI PRIMO

IN MUSÆO BRITANNICO

COLLOCARI JUSSIT.

This has been thought by many scholars to compare favourably with the inscription which was actually adopted and placed in the King's library.

Sir Henry Halford's intimate professional friend, Dr. Matthew Baillie, with whom he had shared the best medical business of the town, and his colleague for many years in attendance first on the Princess Amelia, and then on George III., died in September, 1823. On that and some subsequent occasions it was insinuated rather than absolutely stated, that a jealousy had existed between these two celebrated physicians, and a lack of sincerity on the part of Sir Henry towards his distinguished colleague. But of any such feeling there is neither record nor ground for suspicion in the papers before me. On the contrary, they all go to show the sincerity and kindness of feeling that existed on the part of Sir Henry Halford towards Dr. Baillie.

Baillie and Halford were contemporaries of about the same age and standing, and therefore in a manner necessarily rivals—friendly and honourable rivals—in their profession. Perhaps, too, they represented different schools in that profession, but they always lived in the utmost harmony, and a warm friendship and a close and intimate relation subsisted between them from the time, 1809, when they were called in together to attend the Princess Amelia. There is ample evidence in confidential letters to Sir Henry Halford from members of the Royal Family, especially from the Princess Mary, a constant and close observer of all that passed, showing the harmony of opinion, the intimacy of the friendship, and the perfect mutual confidence that subsisted between Sir Henry Halford and Dr. Baillie.

Among Sir Henry Halford's papers, there are three letters inclosed in one envelope and endorsed in his own writing: "My three last letters from Baillie "—" Alas! my friend, my brother."   They are as follow:

"TUNBRIDGE WELLS, *July 8th*, 1823.

" MY DEAR SIR HENRY,

     " Your letter of to-day has been a great cordial to me, and I send you my warmest thanks for it.   The new College* will now be completed in as handsome a manner as the dignity of that body requires, and this may be said to be entirely owing to your zeal, to your exertions and the influence of your public situation and character. This must form a memorial of you, as lasting as the new College itself, and which indeed can never perish.   The first time that I go to the College I will subscribe my name as approving

---

* It will be observed that at this time Sir Henry was already president of the College of Physicians, and had effected the removal of the building, which was then in progress, from its obscure situation in the City to the best site in London.

of the terms of sale, if this proceeding is not irregular.

"My cough is better, but still continues severe. My appetite is not improving. I shall therefore return to town early next week that I may see more of you before you leave town.

"Yours most truly,

"M. BAILLIE.

"To Sir HENRY HALFORD, Curzon Street."

"CAVENDISH SQUARE,
"*Wednesday, July 22nd,* 1823.

"MY DEAR SIR HENRY,

"I have now been in London a week and propose to set off for Gloucestershire by very easy journeys. I am on the whole a very little better than when I last saw you in London. My cough is less frequent, and I am perhaps a little less listless. I have no appetite whatever, but my tongue is rather less furred, and once or twice I have eat my dinner with rather less reluctance. The same plan of medicine has been continued by Maton since you left town. When I have been two or three days in Gloucestershire I shall write to you again.

"I hope that you are enjoying yourself in the country as you deserve, and that your daughter's confinement is going on favourably. I find that I still experience considerable difficulty in the management of my pen. I send you again my sincerest thanks for all your kindness, and I remain,

"My dearest Sir Henry,

"Yours most truly,

"M. BAILLIE.

"Sir HENRY HALFORD, Wistow, Market Harborough."

"DUNTISBOURNE, Saturday, September 20th.

"MY DEAR SIR HENRY,

"I have within these few days become so very much worse, that, if not very inconvenient to you, I should be glad to see you at my house. Dr. Baron of Gloucester, who is in regular attendance, and I never knew a more skilful and kind-hearted man, will meet you at my house if you are able to come.

"Believe me, dear Sir Henry,

"Yours most sincerely,

"M. BAILLIE."

To this was added—

"As a postscript, I am desired by Dr. Baron to inform you of some of the symptoms which at present exist. There is swelling of the left foot and hand, and at times considerable confusion of intellect. The pulse is seldom under 100, frequently more. The tongue and fauces have been repeatedly covered with aphthæ, and the exhaustion of strength and emaciation increase rapidly. The aversion to food is not quite so great as it has been, but there is nothing taken with any relish, and what has been taken for a long time past seems in no respect to have nourished the body. The affection of the trachea seems nearly removed, and saving occasional tightness and wandering pains about the chest, the organs of respiration are perfectly free. The foregoing detail will sufficiently show how urgent the case is, and how needful it is to afford any relief that may be administered as speedily as possible.

"W. H. BAILLIE."[*]

Sir Henry complied with his friend's request, and started immediately from Wistow for Duntis-bourne, but the post, especially across country, was then slow, and travelling difficult, and he arrived too late. Dr. Baillie died on Tuesday, 23rd September, 1823.

These letters are in proof of Dr. Baillie's feeling towards Sir Henry Halford, and of his entire trust and confidence in him, both as friend and as physician. Dr. Baillie selects Sir Henry from among the whole of the medical profession in London to attend him in his last illness, and when *in extremis* he appeals to him to come to his aid. Written as these letters were, by a man distin-

---

[*] The signature of Dr. Baillie's only son.

guished for the sincerity of his character, and the plainness of his speech ; to one whom he had the best means of estimating at his true worth, they are especially valuable and interesting.

That these feelings were reciprocated by Sir Henry Halford is certain ; and he gave eloquent expression to them in the eulogium he pronounced on the character of his departed friend and colleague from the chair of the College of Physicians in December, 1823. Having announced the bequests contained in Dr. Baillie's will, consisting, amongst others, of his medical library to the College, he continued :

" The same principles which guided Dr. Baillie in his private and domestic life, governed his public and professional behaviour. He was kind, generous and sincere. His purse and his personal services were always at the command of those who could prefer a proper claim to them ; and every branch of the profession met with equal attention. Nay, such was his condescension that he often incurred great inconvenience to himself, by his punctual observance of appointments with the humblest practitioners.

" In consultation he was candid and liberal in the highest degree ; and so industriously gave credit to the previous treatment of the patient (if he could approve of it), that the physician who called him in never failed to find himself in the same possession of the good opinion of the family, as he was before the circumstances of the case had made a consultation necessary.

" His manner of explaining the disease, and the remedies recommended, was peculiar to himself, and singularly happy. It was a short compressed lecture, in which the objects in view, and the means by which they were to be obtained, were developed with great clearness of conception, and in such simple unadorned language as was intelligible to his patient and satisfactory to his colleague.

" Before his time, it was not usual for a physician to do much more than prescribe remedies for the malady, and to encourage the patient by such arguments of consolation as might present themselves to humane and cultivated minds. But as the assumed gravity and outward signs of the profession were now considered obsolete customs, and were, by general consent, laid aside by the physicians, and as a more curious anxiety began to be observed on the part of the patient to learn everything connected with his complaint, arising naturally from the improved state of general knowledge, a different conduct became necessary in the sick-room. The innovation required by the spirit of modern times never could have been adopted by any one more fitted by nature and inclination to carry it into effect than by Dr. Baillie.

"The attention which he paid to morbid anatomy (that alteration of structure which parts have undergone by disease) enabled him to make a nice discrimination in symptoms, and to distinguish between disorders which resemble each other. It gave him a confidence also in propounding his opinions, which our conjectural art does not readily admit ; and the reputation which he enjoyed universally for openness and sincerity made his *dicta* be received with a ready and unresisting faith.

"He appeared to lay a great stress upon the information which he might derive from the external examination of his patient, and to be much influenced in the formation of his opinion of the nature of the complaint, by this practice. He had originally adopted this habit from the peculiar turn of his early studies ; and assuredly such a method, not indiscriminately but judiciously employed, as he employed it, is a valuable auxiliary to the other ordinary means used by a physician of obtaining the knowledge of a disease submitted to him. But it is equally true that, notwithstanding its air of mechanical precision, such examination is not to be depended upon beyond a certain point. Great disordered action may prevail in a part without having produced such disorganisation as may be sensibly felt; and to doubt of the existence of a disease because it is not discoverable by the touch, is not only unphilosophical, but must surely, in many instances, lead to unfounded and erroneous conclusions. One of the inevitable consequences of such a system is frequent disappointment in foretelling the issue of the malady, that most important of all points to the reputation of a physician; and though such a mode of investigation might prove eminently successful in the skilful hands of Dr. Baillie, it must be allowed to be an example of dangerous tendency to those who have not had his means of acquiring knowledge, nor enjoyed the advantages of his great experience, nor have learned, by the previous steps of education and good discipline, to reason and judge correctly. The quickness with which a physician of keen perception and great practice makes up his mind on the nature of a disease, and the plan of treatment to be employed, differs as widely as possible from the inconsiderate haste which marks the decisions of the rash and the uninformed. . . . . .

" But justice cannot be done to Dr. Baillie's

medical character, unless that important feature
in it which appeared in every part of his conduct
and demeanour, his religious principle, be distinctly
stated and recognised.   His ample converse with
one of the most wonderful works of the Creator—
the formation of man—inspired in him an admiration of the Supreme Being which nothing could
exceed.   He had, indeed, 'looked through nature
up to nature's God'; and the promises of the
Gospel, on the conditions explained by our
Redeemer, were his humble but confident hope in
life and his consolation in death.

"If one precept appeared to be more practically approved by him than another, it was that
which directs us to do unto others as we would
have them do unto us; and this was felt and
acknowledged daily by all his professional
brethren in their intercourse with him.   On the
whole, we may say of him, what Tacitus does of
Agricola—'Bonum virum facile crederes; magnum
libenter.'"

Having read the above eulogium, Sir Henry
Halford proposed to the College that a bust of
Dr. Baillie by Chantrey should be obtained and
placed in a prominent position in the new
College, which was unanimously agreed to.

It is true nevertheless that when, shortly after

Dr. Baillie's death, a proposal was made by Dr. Pelham Warren and some of his friends to pay honour to Baillie's memory by a monument in Westminster Abbey it was discountenanced by Sir Henry Halford ; but only because, as he was careful to explain, he thought a display of this kind unsuited to the profession of a physician. Moreover, that the most fitting mode of doing honour to Baillie was that adopted by the College of Physicians, the placing of his bust among those of such ornaments of English physic as Harvey, Sydenham and Mead. At a subsequent period, Sir Henry, actuated by like feelings, was opposed to the erection of the monument to Dr. Babington in St. Paul's Cathedral.

When Sir Henry Halford was in closest attendance on the Court, as he was during the reign of George IV., he found it necessary to have at hand, one among his fellow physicians residing in his immediate neighbourhood on whom he could rely, and to whom he might depute such of his professional work, as at the moment he himself was unable to perform. He fixed, in the first instance, on Dr. Turner of Curzon Street, long treasurer of the College of Physicians, and next, when that physician withdrew from practice, on Dr. Macmichael of Half-moon Street, a man of many accomplishments who had travelled much, and with whom Sir Henry maintained a close intimacy and warm friendship, until Dr. Macmichael was struck down with paralysis in 1836. To Dr. Macmichael succeeded Dr. Francis Hawkins of Curzon Street, the first professor of medicine in King's College, London, who had married a daughter of Mr. Justice Vaughan, and a niece therefore of Sir Henry Halford. He continued to occupy this position to the last, and was himself in medical attendance on Sir Henry throughout the illness which proved fatal to him.

During this and the previous decade, Sir Henry Halford was in the fullest exercise of his profession, all the highest duties of which are performed in the privacy of the sick chamber. The more successful a physician is therefore, and the more he is engaged in the highest duties of his office, the less is there to meet observation or to court publicity, and the less material consequently for biography. "The physician's part," writes Johnson, "lies hid in domestic privacy, and silent duties and silent excellences are soon forgotten." So it was in the case of Sir Henry Halford, and there is little of special character or interest to record concerning him during the later portion of his life. The following are the only ones personal to himself, and as distinguished from the College of Physicians and his attendance on the Royal Family; and these form the subjects of special chapters hereafter.

In June, 1831, when the advent of Asiatic cholera to this country appeared to be imminent, the government sought first from Sir Henry Halford, and next from the College of Physicians, information regarding the disease itself, and advice as to the means of preventing its entrance amongst us. The Privy Council was already in possession of much documentary evidence concerning the disease, which had been supplied by consuls and ministers abroad. At the instance of Lord Lansdowne and Lord Auckland, Sir Henry Halford was sent for, all these papers were placed in his hands, and he was desired to report as speedily as possible, whether the disease was contagious, and whether it could be conveyed by goods? He reported next day; *yes*, to the first question, but *no* to the second.* The whole subject with all the papers, was next submitted to

* "The Greville Memoirs," edited by Henry Reeve, first series, vol. ii. p. 151 *et seq.*

the College of Physicians, which so far departed from the opinion of Sir Henry Halford, as to affirm that the disease could be conveyed by goods.   A Board of Health was next formed.   It was constituted of twelve persons, six of whom besides Sir Henry Halford, who was declared president of the board, were fellows of the College of Physicians.   To them were added the comptroller of the Navy, the deputy-chairman of the Customs, the director-general of Army Hospitals, the medical commissioner of the Victualling Office, and the superintendent-general of Quarantine.

The Board of Health so constituted considered very carefully the several questions before it.   It declared its conviction of the contagious nature of the disease, and recommended the establishment of a system of strict quarantine.   But this was not in accord with the views or intentions of government, especially in regard to quarantine, and it was thought fit under such circumstances to dissolve the existing Board of Health and constitute another in its place.   While this change was in contemplation, Sir Henry Halford on the part of the Board of Health addressed the following explanation to the Privy Council :

"The Board of Health has proceeded silently but usefully it believes, to accomplish the objects expected by the Privy Council from its establishment.

"After an industrious perusal of all the documents it could meet with relating to the progress of the Indian cholera, it gave a decided opinion without compromise, that it was an infectious disease.

"This led to a respectful representation on its part, that an inexorable quarantine should be established ; for the malady it appeared had been imported into the Mauritius—it had been imported at a subsequent period into the port of Dantzic, and other harbours of the Baltic ; and if it reached this country it must be *imported* here.

"The board moreover took great pains to acquire an accurate knowledge of the symptoms of the disease, misappropriately called cholera morbus ; and having acquired this, by a careful perusal of the India reports, and by a personal examination of different Indian practitioners and of physicians who had seen the disease in Europe, was enabled to promulgate so clear an account of it, as precluded the possibility of confounding it with the cholera of this country. It has thereby prevented much anxiety and a great deal of unnecessary alarm.

"They have further exercised their judgment upon the various modes of treating the disease, and by discountenancing absurd methods of cure,

have saved the country from the reproach
and danger of adopting rash and mischievous
remedies.

" The board has besides recommended the
establishment of local boards in the country and
over England generally, to whom they are now
giving the best instruction in their power.

" They were prepared moreover to take upon
themselves the responsibility of any additional
measures which they might think it expedient to
recommend, if in their intercourse with the sick
[should this disease fall upon this country and
prevail generally] they should be able to discover
an approved mode of practice.

" They are now about to turn their attention to
one of the most important points of the disease,
namely, how long its contagion lies dormant in the
body—upon which hinges the great question of
the proper duration of quarantine.

" If the board be dissolved prematurely, there
would be no body to appeal to, and every man in
the kingdom must be reduced to think and act for
himself.

" HENRY HALFORD."

[No date.]

But the " Board of Health " was superseded
and then dissolved. On the 2nd November,
1831, a "Central Board of Health" was instituted
in its place. This was very differently constituted
to the original board and it failed to secure the

confidence of the medical profession, or of the public at large. Sir Henry Halford was not connected with it, nor was a single fellow of the College of Physicians placed on this new board. The new board consisted of the Hon. Edward R. Stewart, chairman, Sir William Pym, K.C.H., Lieut.-Col. John Marshall, Dr. Russell, Dr. Barry, K.T.S., Major R. Macdonald, and William Maclean, secretary. The Central Board professed the same general opinion of the infectious nature of cholera as had the General Board, but it shortened the duration of quarantine, and at once declared against all coercive attempts to isolate the disease. Its further history would be out of place here.

Lady Halford died 17th June, 1833. Her last illness and death is the subject of one or two letters of sympathy and condolence from Sir Henry Halford's friends, but I fail to find in his own notes anything concerning his loss—if such existed they were probably destroyed. I fail too, to gather any information personal or traditional of Lady Halford from other sources. She died sixty years since and I can hear of no one, who has sufficient recollection of her, to aid me. According to the elegant inscription to her memory at Wistow, from the pen of Sir Henry Halford, she was " distinguished by the graces and accomplishments which became a descent from a long line of noble ancestors, she was exemplary in the discharge of all her duties, studious to promote the welfare and happiness of all around her, remarkable for sincerity of character, humble before God, charitable to mankind, a most affectionate wife and tender mother."

In October, 1833, Sir Henry Halford was admitted to an "ad eundem" degree at Cambridge. The address of the public orator Dr. Tatham, on presenting him for that honour, was felt by Sir Henry and his friends who were present, to be so true and withal so elegantly expressed, that they were anxious to obtain a written copy of it, but Dr. Tatham felt obliged to decline to give it. In a letter to a friend he says it was most gratifying to him to learn that when he had the honour and pleasure of presenting Sir Henry Halford for the degree, he was so fortunate in the selection of the topics as to give satisfaction to that "accomplished scholar." But, he continues, "as these slight effusions are not intended to be *oculis subjecta* but merely *demissa per aurem*, I hope you will not think that I am insensible either to Sir Henry Halford's indulgent partiality or to your own great kindness."

In reference to Sir Henry's visits to Cambridge about and at this period, there is the following letter from the chancellor of the university, his friend and patient the Duke of Gloucester. It is interesting as alluding to the very last effort which Sir Henry Halford made, to maintain the time-honoured connection between the English universities of Oxford and Cambridge and the College of Physicians of London.

"GLOUCESTER HOUSE, *Aug.* 2, '33.

"MY DEAR SIR HENRY,

"I hasten to return to you my best thanks for the very obliging letter, I had this morning the pleasure of receiving from you, by which, I am exceedingly glad to find that you are so well satisfied with your visit to *our* university as I trust I may now consider you as belonging to us. I greatly lament that I shall not have the opportunity of conferring your degree ad eundem in person, as I had always flattered myself would have been the case, and which was so near taking place in 1828, but under existing circumstances I think you judge perfectly right in determining to be admitted in October.

"The account you so kindly give me of what occurred during the two days you passed at Cambridge, you will readily believe affords me sincerest gratification, and I very sensibly feel all you have the goodness to say. Your meeting with the vice-chancellor, the master of St. John's and Dr. Haviland will be attended with the most useful consequences, and most highly do I approve of the plan you have agreed upon. There is now a perfect understanding. The universities will maintain what is essential to themselves; the College of Physicians will have what they ought to have; and we shall prevent power being given where it ought not to exist.

"I am ever with the truest friendship, esteem and respect,

"My dear Sir Henry,

"Very sincerely yours,

"WILLIAM FREDERICK."

In 1835 two eminent London physicians died, Dr. Maton and Dr. Pelham Warren, both of whom had been in extensive practice among the upper classes, and after the death of Dr. Baillie had shared with Sir Henry Halford the best medical business of the town. Sir Henry was thus left for a time the undisputed master of the situation. Dr. Chambers, it is true, succeeded in time to much of the business of these two physicians and eventually to the position they had occupied in relation to Sir Henry Halford.

Sir Henry's long tenure of his position at

Court, and of the best medical business of the town, which had now lasted over more than a quarter of a century, became the subject of talk and perhaps of envy among his juniors, and led among others, to the following *jeu d'esprit*, commonly attributed to Dr. Paris:

> " 'Tis said that death no favor shows
> But strikes alike both friends and foes,
>   Without a predilection;
> Why strikes he then those men of art
> Whose skill so oft has foiled his dart,
>   As if 'twere by selection?
> While he alone whose courtly smiles
> Can charm away all human ails
>   Is left on earth to tarry:
> No, certain 'tis, that death well knows,
> Who are his friends and who his foes,
>   And therefore spares Sir Harry."

In the autumn of 1838, an event occurred which all persons interested in Sir Henry Halford must lament. His friend and neighbour Mr. Lockley, a much respected medical practitioner, of Half-moon Street, when on his way along with Sir Henry to stay with him at Wistow, was seized with apoplexy in the railway carriage, and at Tring was removed from it into the station-house. Sir Henry ordered a surgeon to be immediately sent for, and having directed what he should do on his arrival, left Mr. Lockley and proceeded on his journey to Wistow. These circumstances not unnaturally exposed Sir Henry to much adverse criticism in the periodical press, and it is believed cast a gloom over some of the later years of his life. As the only direct and authoritative account of the circumstances as they occurred, is contained in a letter from Sir Henry Halford to the *Times* newspaper, that letter is subjoined :

" *To the Editor of* THE TIMES.

" SIR,—I have been appealed to, in such terms as I cannot resist, to give some account of the circumstances attending the death of Mr. Lockley. Here is the unvarnished tale :

" Mr. Lockley had been unwell in the spring of the year, but had recovered in the summer. Believing that a change of air and of scene might do him good, I invited him to accompany me on my next visit into Leicestershire, and we set out the following morning, the 2nd of October. We proceeded to Euston Square, where Mr. Lockley had a fall, but he assured me repeatedly, in answer to my urgent questions, whether he were ill, or had fallen by mere accident, that it was merely an accident.

" When we had passed Watford, Mr. Lockley became sick, and soon afterwards fell asleep, breathed oppressively, and did not answer to my questions. In this state, when we arrived at

Tring, I took him out of the carriage and carried him into the parlour of the inspector of that station, a most humane person, who sent off instantly by my desire, to Mr. Dewsbury of Tring, a medical practitioner of much credit and business there, desiring him to come, or to send his assistant immediately to Mr. Lockley's aid. I gave directions what should be done, and requested further that Mr. Dewsbury, when he had bled Mr. Lockley, would send a message to London, to apprise his family of the misfortune, and to request Dr. Lockley, his son, to come down immediately. Having given these directions, I felt I could not be of any further use at present, and therefore pursued my journey. Mr. Dewsbury executed all my wishes within an hour, and Dr. Lockley arrived at ten o'clock the same evening.

" I should have been ready to return the next day, but after Mr. Dewsbury's first visit, Mr. Lockley had the daily assistance of friends from London, and Dr. Watson gave his sanction to his patient's removal to London on the 6th, which I learned by a letter from Mrs. Lockley, the following day, informing me that he had accomplished the journey without inconvenience and was thought better. If I could have administered, instead of directing only the expedients of our art to my friend, I should have done so, but feeling assured that I had provided Mr. Dewsbury's or his assistant's immediate attention, I went on ; and my conscience does not reproach me with the slightest neglect of my friend, who died, not that evening, as has been erroneously stated, but on the 14th of October, twelve days after the first seizure, in the bosom of his family in Half-moon Street.

"I am, Sir, much your servant,

"HENRY HALFORD.

"CURZON STREET, *November* 5."

All must admit that Sir Henry committed a grave error in leaving his friend insensible, in the hands of strangers at a railway station ; and all must wish that on subsequent reflection it had been frankly admitted to have been so. But it was not. The wisest of men have their moments of indiscretion, and Sir Henry Halford was but another instance of that truth.

Sir Henry Halford's early success in the practice of his profession, left him but little leisure for composition.   His essays in the "Medical Transactions of the College of Physicians," on the "Climacteric Disease" and on the "Necessity of Caution in the Estimation of Symptoms in the last steps of some Diseases :" and those on "Tic Douloureux ;" on the "Phlegmasia Dolens ;" and on the "Treatment of Gout," the most important of the strictly medical writings from his pen. are of a character to make us regret that his contributions to our professional literature were not more numerous. His other "Essays" were read at the evening meetings of the College of Physicians, before a mixed assemblage, and are therefore of a somewhat popular character. They were admirably adapted to the occasion, and they afford abundant proof of Sir Henry's elegant taste and classical attainments. His two Harveian orations, and his oration on the opening of the new College of Physicians in Pall Mall East, are models of Latin composition.

As his professional work diminished—it did so after the death of William IV.—he betook himself again and with unabated interest to those pursuits which had been his delight at Oxford. In imitation of his friends, the Marquis Wellesley and Lord Granville, he turned to the composition of Latin poetry, chiefly in his carriage, and so beguiled the tedium of many a long day spent in his professional pursuits. This resource, he tells us, was suggested to him in a conversation with Lord Granville ; who, after having been occupied incessantly in politics for nearly thirty years, was seized by illness and confined to his armchair a great part of the remainder of his life. In this state Sir Henry always found him not tranquil and cheerful only, as might have been expected from his habitual piety, but amused : and on Sir Henry asking him the secret of this happy peculiarity he answered, " I go back to my classics, sir." The next day Lord Granville sent Sir Henry a copy of his " Nugæ Metricæ," containing original exercises and translations. Sir Henry thought he could not do better than imitate such an example, and provide himself with a similar resource, whenever his own power of further exertion should be terminated by age, or interrupted by such disease as might leave him in possession of his faculties.

Sir Henry's own " Nugæ Metricæ," printed and published in 1842, was the result. The pieces, in number thirty-six, bespeak a happy facility of composition and a correct taste. As specimens of them I select the two following, which were specially commended by Lord Wellesley, a very competent authority. The first consists of lines, suggested by Haydon's picture of Buonaparte, in the possession of Sir Robert Peel. Buonaparte is there represented as standing at the edge of the rock at St. Helena, with his arms folded, contemplating a white sail in the horizon. His back is toward the spectator—the sun setting.

> " Tristis, iners, solusque abrupto in limite rupis,
>   Stat circumspiciens Exul, si fortè ratem quam

Unda vehat, reditûs spem, perfugiumque ferentem.
Circùm cuncta silent, non vox, non murmura ponti
Percepta, occiduas dum Sol se condit in undas.
Ah miser! Ille diem referens vitamque resurget
Splendidior cras, mane novo.　Tu sanguine fuso,
Criminibusque satur, solio detrusus ab alto,
Divulsusque tuis, veluti sub rupe Prometheus
Fixus inaccessâ, morbo vexatus et irâ
Conficiêre, miser! mortemque optabis acerbam."

The following, specially commended by Lord Wellesley as "a proof of great power of Latinity," is a translation of the song in Sheridan's " Duenna ":

" Si violare fidem mihi cor proclivius esset,
　　Crede mihi, me non posse nocere tibi.
Quamquam etenim tua verba fidem me nulla rogâssent,
　　Fecissent fidum forma decusque tuum.

Ergo pone metus, et fraudem parce vereri,
　　Neu timeas fictos in tua damna dolos :
Cunctos nempe senes inter numerabis amicos,
　　Nec juvenis, qui te non amet, ullus erit.

Et cum te socio tandem devinxeris uni,
　　Protenùs ardentes, cætera turba, proci,
Demittent æstum stimulosque Cupidinis omnes,
　　Fraternæque dabunt pignora amicitiæ." *

* Sheridan's original is as follows :

　　　" Had I a heart for falsehood framed,
　　　　I ne'er could injure you,
　　　For tho' your tongue no promise claim'd,
　　　　Your charms would make me true.

　　　Then, Lady, dread not here deceit,
　　　　Nor fear to suffer wrong,
　　　For friends in all the aged you'll meet,
　　　　And lovers in the young.

The last piece of the collection is in English, and for that reason may be added. It is an inscription for a mausoleum :

> "Stranger ! by curious contemplation led,
>   Whoe'er thou art, this solemn scene to tread,
>   May no compunctious visitings annoy,
>   No unrepented sins thy peace destroy,—
>   No passing day wound with a Parthian dart,—
>   But ev'ry hour fresh blessedness impart !
>   Yet,—should some vice, indulged without control,
>   Peril thy future bliss, enthral thy soul,
>   O ! go not hence, till thou hast sternly vow'd
>   To sin no more—to thy Creator bow'd
>   In contrite sorrow, and His aid implored,
>   Who died—that sinful man to God might be restored."

Sir Henry Halford had been blessed with a good constitution which had never been injured by excesses of any kind. He was moderate in the use of wine, and this at a time when temperance was scarcely thought to be a virtue. He enjoyed excellent health, and passed through a long, laborious and anxious life without serious illness of any kind. His health and energy continued indeed without any very marked abatement up to about his seventy-fifth year, when they began to fail him. He continued in practice until within a few months of his death. He had

> And when they find that you have bless'd
>   Another with your heart,
> They'll bid aspiring passion rest,
>   And act a brother's part."

suffered for some time from occasional attacks
of pain, in the course of the nerves of the upper
and lower extremities of the left side, and had
become visibly thinner. The pains had after a
time increased in intensity and some five or six
months before his death, had assumed all the
characters of tic douloureux ; his sufferings from
which, neither his own large experience and
fertility of resources, nor the best efforts of his
friends, Dr. Seymour of St. George's hospital and
Dr. Francis Hawkins who attended him, were
able materially to alleviate ; and which were
temporarily and partially only relieved by full
doses of opium.

In sequel to pain and the loss of sleep consequent thereon, the powers of his stomach gave
way ; emaciation and debility progressively increased, and notwithstanding every effort on the
part of his medical attendants, to support him, he
expired in a state of extreme exhaustion, at his
house in Curzon Street, on the 9th March, 1844,
aged seventy-seven.

His body was removed to Wistow and buried
in the church there, which already contained the
remains of his father and mother, of his wife, and
of his brother Justice Vaughan. In the church
there is a mural monument to his memory with

the following inscription from the pen of his friend, Dr. Francis Hawkins; revised (as I was told by Dr. Hawkins himself) by Dr. Copleston, the bishop of Llandaff and dean of St. Paul's, but perhaps better known as the distinguished provost of Oriel College, Oxford.

HENRICO HALFORD, BARONETTO G.C.H.

EX ÆDE CHRISTI APUD OXONIENSES M.D.

JACOBI VAUGHAN, MEDICI CLARI

FILIO CLARIORI :

QUI SOBRINI SUI CAROLI HALFORD BARONETTI

(EIDEM ORDINI ET IPSE ADSCRIPTUS)

HÆREDITATEM EX TESTAMENTO ET NOMEN SUSCEPIT.

MEDICORUM COLL : REG : LONDIN :

CUM PLAUSU ET FAVORE OMNIUM ANNOS XXIV PRÆFUIT.

REGUM GEORGII III. GEORGII IV. GULIELMI IV.

MEDICUS ORDINARIUS.

NECNON A PLERISQUE EJUSDEM STIRPIS PRINCIPIBUS

IN OPEM FAMILIARITER VOCATUS.

AD MORBOS DIJUDICANDOS SAGAX, AD SUBLEVANDOS POLLENS,

INGENII ACUMINE, REMEDIORUM COPIÁ, PARITER INSIGNIS,

ARTEM QUAM MORIBUS ORNABAT

LATÈ ET FELICITER EXERCEBAT.

LITERIS HUMANIORIBUS ADMODUM IMBUTUS

VIXIT OMNIBUS ACCEPTUS, ERGA OMNES BENEVOLUS,

NATUS DIE OCTOBRIS IJ. A.S. MDCCLXVI.

OBIIT DIE MART. IX. A.S. MDCCCXLIV,

IN SOLO SALUTIS AUCTORE JESU CHRISTO

SPEM VITÆ IMMORTALIS OMNEM COLLOCAVIT.

FILIUS GRATUS PIUS

H.M. FAC. CUR.

Sir Henry Halford had one son and one

daughter. His son Henry, born 22nd April, 1797, married his first cousin Barbara, the second daughter of Sir John Vaughan, one of the barons of the Exchequer. He for many years represented South Leicestershire in Parliament, succeeded as the second baronet, and died 22nd May, 1868—his relict died 24th June, 1869. Louisa, the only daughter of Sir Henry Halford, Bart., was married 18th October, 1819 to Frederick, the eldest son of the Honourable John Coventry. She died 30th September, 1865.

Sir Henry Halford's will, made shortly after Lady Halford's death, and dated the 18th September, 1833, is written by himself. It was witnessed by his three medical friends, Dr. Macmichael, Dr. Thomas Turner, and Dr. John Bright, and is as follows :

" In the name of God, Amen. I, Sir Henry Halford, Baronet, of Wistow Hall, in the county of Leicester, being of sound and disposing mind, do make this my last will and testament.

" I give and bequeath to my dear son, Henry Halford, his heirs, executors and assigns and administrators, all my real and personal estate whatsoever and wheresoever to be found. And I do hereby appoint him my sole executor.

" In testimony whereof I affix my signature and

my seal this eighteenth of September, in the presence of the three several witnesses, whose names are underwritten.

HENRY HALFORD, Bart. (L.S.)

" Signed, sealed, published and declared to be the last will and testament of the same Sir Henry Halford, Bart., by him in our presence this eighteenth day of September, in the year of our Lord 1833.

WILLIAM MACMICHAEL, M.D.
THOMAS TURNER, M.D.
JOHN BRIGHT, M.D."

It was proved 1st April, 1844, when his effects were sworn under £9000, but in May, 1846, they were resworn as under £16,000.

CHAPTER VI

THE College of Physicians, in the year 1793, when
Sir Henry Halford joined it, and for thirty years
after, was situated within the city, in Warwick
Lane, Newgate Street. There he had repeatedly
served the office of censor, and there he had
delivered the Harveian oration of 1800.

At that time, and subsequently, throughout the
whole of his life, even when most oppressed by the
duties of his extensive business, Sir Henry was
attentive to the interests of the College, and ready
to devote himself, his energies and his influence,
to the furtherance of its welfare and the mainte-
nance of its dignity. On the 30th September,
1820, he was elected president of the College,
and at once applied himself to the removal of
the corporation from the city to the west end
of the town, an object which the fellows had

long had much at heart, but had not dared to encounter.

To the College in Warwick Lane, capacious as it was, convenient in its internal arrangement, and as a whole imposing in appearance, there was the one serious drawback of its situation. In the period that had elapsed since its erection, great changes had taken place in London and especially in the city. The immediate neighbourhood of the College had greatly deteriorated; population and fashion had moved westward, and the situation of the College, always bad, and the only approach to it through Warwick Lane, narrow and difficult, became year by year more inconvenient. Everything concurred to show the advisability of removal to a more convenient situation. Various attempts had been made from time to time in this direction, but each had proved abortive.

In 1814 the College obtained an Act of Parliament to enable it to hold its corporate meetings and exercise its powers within the city of Westminster and its liberties. And now, mainly through Sir Henry Halford's personal influence with the prime minister, the Earl of Liverpool, and with the highest personage in the realm, a grant of land in Pall Mall East, on which the College now stands, valued then at six thousand pounds, was obtained from the crown ;* and on it the present College, designed by Sir Robert Smirke, was forthwith commenced. The old premises in Warwick Lane were sold for nine thousand pounds. The Radcliffe trustees gave two thousand pounds towards the cost of the new building. And what was needed in addition, and it was much—for the building and fittings cost more than twenty-five thousand pounds over and above the funds which had been accumulating for some years for this purpose—was subscribed by the loans and liberal contributions of the fellows of the College themselves. But many years elapsed before the entire cost of the edifice was liquidated.

It was at this time, whilst the College house was in course of erection, and the fellows were without a fitting place to meet in, that the king— George IV.—was pleased to confer a high honour on the College of Physicians, and to testify his

* It was then granted for a lease of ninety-nine and a half years only ; but on the 25th July, 1864, an Act of Parliament, to enable her Majesty to grant a lease for nine hundred and ninety-nine years, received the royal sanction, and the seal of the College was affixed to the lease in the Comitia Majora of the 30th September, 1865.

appreciation of the character and abilities of its president, Sir Henry Halford. The king was pleased in the following letter to declare that the president of the College for the time being, should ex-officio hold the office of physician-in-ordinary to his Majesty :

" The King desires Sir Henry Halford as president of the Royal College of Physicians to announce to the College assembled, that it is the king's pleasure in future, that the president for the time being, should always hold the office of physician-in-ordinary to his Majesty. The king has great pleasure in making this communication during Sir Henry's presidency, from the sincere regard he entertains for him, and the very high estimation in which he holds his character and abilities.

"G. R.

"CARLTON HOUSE, *January 18th*, 1822."

The College replied in the following humble address :

" *To the King's Most Excellent Majesty.*

" SIRE,

"We, the President, Elects and Fellows of the Royal College of Physicians, humbly approach your Majesty with our most grateful acknowledgments for the mark of royal favour with which your Majesty has been pleased to distinguish us, by an order written and signed by your royal hand addressed to Sir Henry Halford, Bart., our president, commanding him to declare to the College assembled your Majesty's royal will and pleasure, that every future president of the College of Physicians for the time being shall hold the office of one of your Majesty's physicians-in-ordinary.

" We associate, Sire, with this mark of your royal kindness, the pleasing remembrance of the circumstances of our original foundation by your Majesty's illustrious predecessor King Henry VIII., and dare to presume from so gracious a proof of your confidence in us, that your Majesty entertains a favourable opinion of our institutions and discipline, as calculated to make our profession respected in this country, above what it is in any other part of Europe, and most capable of forming a physician worthy to be placed near the sacred person of the king.

" To our president, Sire, we entrust this expression of our dutiful thanks, our loyalty, and our attachment and devotion to your Majesty, and we pray that no weight of cares which your Majesty's great office imposes upon you may prove injurious to your health, and that Providence in its infinite goodness may continue to watch over a life so highly important to the welfare and happiness of your kingdoms."

The College addressed the president as follows :

"*February* 1st, 1822.

" SIR,

"The fellows of the Royal College of Physicians embrace with the greatest pleasure this opportunity of expressing their warmest thanks to the president for his uniform attention to the duties of his important office, and the zeal which he has uniformly displayed in promoting the interests of the College. They are, however, in a more especial manner impressed with a deep sense of gratitude on account of the very high honour, *which through his means*, his Majesty has been graciously pleased to confer upon the College, in appointing the president for the time being to be always ex-officio one of his Majesty's physicians-in-ordinary. This cannot fail to be a great advantage to the College, and is a higher honour than has ever been conferred upon it by any prior sovereign. They finally express an ardent wish that the president may long enjoy good health to be enabled to perform with his usual ability his duties to the College and to the public." *

* It was thought from the king's letter, that the privilege thereby conferred on the president of the College of Physicians would be of perpetual obligation and binding on his successors. So it was certainly understood by Sir Henry Halford. But when Dr. Paris had been elected president, and as such, applied to be placed among the physicians-in-ordinary to the sovereign, it was held by the Queen's advisers that the command

Soon after this the king commanded, through Sir Henry Halford, that Dr. Southey, a member

of George IV. was not binding on his successors. Dr. Paris had placed the autograph letter of George IV. in the hands of the First Lord of the Treasury, who returned it with the following letter.

"WHITEHALL, *March 28th*, 1844.

"SIR,

"I beg leave to return to you the accompanying paper, which you placed in my hands. Having made inquiry into the subject to which that paper refers I have ascertained that the policy of appointing the president of the College of Physicians physician-in-ordinary to her Majesty, was brought under the consideration of her Majesty at the period of her accession to the crown, and that adverting to the fact that the election of the president is an annual one and to the propriety of leaving the sovereign an unfettered choice of her physician-in-ordinary, her Majesty was advised to withhold her sanction from the rule to which his Majesty George IV. was willing personally to conform.

"Although Sir Henry Halford was continued physician to her Majesty, it was expressly intimated to him that the appointment was a personal one, and was not conferred in virtue of the arrangement contemplated in the enclosed memorandum.

"It was intended, I believe, that a communication to this effect should have been made at the time to the College of Physicians, but I conclude, as you were not aware of this fact, that it was inadvertently omitted.

"The decision, however, was taken at the period to which I refer and after full consideration, and I trust that you will not consider the adherence to that decision under existing circumstances inconsistent with a sincere respect for that high character, professional and general, which has induced the College of Physicians to confer upon you the distinguished office of president of the College.

"I have the honour to be, Sir,

"Your obedient servant,

"ROBERT PEEL.

"J. A. PARIS, Esq., M.D.,

"President of the College of Physicians."

of the College, should be admitted a fellow, as a preliminary to his appointment as one of the physicians-in-ordinary to his Majesty. Dr. Southey was a younger brother of the poet. He had been a fellow student, at Edinburgh, with the keeper of the privy purse, Sir William Knighton, and a warm and lifelong friendship had been established between them. The appointment of Dr. Southey is known to have been due to the kindly feeling and interposition of Sir William Knighton with the king. As this is the only instance in the history of the College of Physicians, of the exercise of the royal prerogative in this direction, I add the king's letter to Sir Henry Halford on the occasion.

[PRIVATE.]

" The King sends his kind regards to Sir Henry Halford and acquaints him, that it is the king's intention to take an opportunity of appointing Dr. Southey, one of his physicians-in-ordinary, in the room of Sir William Knighton, who has desired, from the heavy pressure of his other situation, to retire from the responsibility of this.

" The king would have been glad if Dr. Southey had been a graduate of either of the English universities, and the king wishes that

Sir Henry would supply this deficiency by making him a fellow of the College. The king mentions this as a continuation of the same feeling, which induced him on a former occasion to state to Sir Henry, that the president of the College of Physicians should in future, for the time being, always be a physician-in-ordinary to the king.

"The king desires to express how sensibly he feels Sir Henry's constant attention, and the benefit which the king at all times derives from his great judgment and skill in his profession.

"G. R.

"C. H., *May 20th*, 1823."

Dr. Southey was admitted a fellow of the College of Physicians 25th June, 1823, and shortly afterwards was gazetted physician-in-ordinary to George IV.

In the course of building the new College, which was attended with much trouble and anxiety to the executive, and especially to the president and treasurer, a strong sense of the services already rendered to the corporation by Sir Henry Halford, sprang up in the breasts of many of the fellows, and it was thought but fit to acknowledge it in some suitable manner.

And so, at a meeting of certain of the fellows of the College held on the 27th May, 1824, at the house of Dr. Turner, the treasurer, Sir Lucas Pepys, Bart., in the chair, it was resolved, "that in the opinion of the meeting, the zeal and ability with which Sir Henry Halford, Bart., has conducted the affairs of the College since he has been president, and the signal success which has resulted from his indefatigable exertions, not only in forwarding the great object of building the new edifice, but in promoting the general welfare and dignity of the College, justly entitle him to the gratitude of all the fellows.

"And that placing his bust among those of former eminent characters and benefactors, at the period of opening the new edifice, would be an appropriate and lasting memorial of the estimation in which he is held by the College."

In order to obtain this object the president was requested to sit to Chantrey for his bust, who had undertaken to finish it in the course of a few months. It was further agreed that the bust when completed should be presented to the College, to be placed at its discretion at the opening of the new building. The funds needed were at once supplied by a subscription of the fellows, and the bust was presented to the College the 4th June, 1825, under which date we read in the Annals :

" Resolved that the bust of the president, Sir Henry Halford, Bart., which has been executed by Chantrey (in consequence of resolutions which passed at a private meeting of the fellows), be accepted by the College and placed among those of former eminent characters and benefactors already in the possession of the College."

It was placed and remains to this day in the censor's room upon a pedestal bearing the line,

Præsenti tibi, maturos largimur honores,

on one side of the door leading to the large library, the bust of his friend and colleague, Dr. Matthew Baillie, being on the other.

The College was opened with due ceremony on the 25th June, 1825, by the president, Sir Henry Halford, who wore the decoration of the royal Guelphic order, which the king had been pleased to confer upon him that morning, and delivered an eloquent Latin oration to an audience, such as in respect of royalty, nobility, official station and learning, had never before, nor has since, been collected in the College.   This important event is recorded in the Annals of the College as follows :

"*Die Junii* 25° 1825.

" On this day the new College was opened.

" At 3 o'clock P.M. the president and fellows, dressed in their doctor's robes, assembled in the censor's room, where they waited to receive the distinguished guests, whom they had invited to be present at the ceremony. Among the visitors who honoured the College with their presence, were the following high personages :

His Royal Highness the Duke of York.
His Royal Highness the Duke of Sussex.
His Royal Highness the Duke of Cambridge.
His Royal Highness the Duke of Gloucester.
His Royal Highness the Prince Leopold.
The Dukes of Grafton, Rutland, Montrose (Lord Chamberlain), Newcastle and Wellington (Master-general of the Ordnance).
The Marquess of Londonderry.
The Earl of Liverpool (First Lord of the Treasury).
The Earl of Westmoreland (Lord Privy Seal).
Earls Grey and Carysfort.
The Earl of Aberdeen (President of the Society of Antiquaries).
Viscounts Sidmouth, Dudley, Deerhurst.
Lord Stowell (Judge of the High Court of Admiralty).
Lords Holland, St. Helens, Henley and Carrington.
The Lord Primate of Ireland.
The Bishops of Lincoln and Chester.
Lord John Russell.
Lord Robert Manners.
The Speaker of the House of Commons.
Count Munster (Hanoverian Minister).
Right Hon. Sir John Nicholl, Knight (Official Principal of Arches Court of Canterbury).
Right Hon. Sir Robert Peel (Secretary of State Home Department).
Right Hon. Frederic Robinson (Chancellor of the Exchequer).
Right Hon. William Huskisson (Treasurer of the Navy).

Right Hon. Charles W. Wynn (President of the Board of Control).

Right Hon. Sir Charles Long (Paymaster of the Forces).

Mr. Dawson and Mr. Hobhouse (Under Secretaries of State for the Home Department).

Right Hon. William Freemantle.

Right Hon. George Tierney, M.P

Right Hon. Thomas Grenville.

Henry Brougham, Esq., M.P.

Sir James Macintosh, M.P.

T. Frank Sotheron, Esq., M.P.

Mr. Banks, M.P.

Mr. Heber, M.P. for the University of Oxford.

Lieut.-Gen. Sir George Walker, G.C.B.

Mr. Mansfield, M.P.

Mr. Serjeant Vaughan.

The Solicitor-General.

William Hamilton, Esq. (His Majesty's late Envoy at the Court of Naples).

Rev. Dr. Goodenough (Head-master of Westminster School).

Rev. Dr. Butler (Head-master of Harrow School).

Rev Dr Maltby (Preacher of Lincoln's Inn).

Rev. Dr. Copleston (Provost of Oriel College, Oxford).

Sir Thomas Lawrence (President of the Royal Academy).

Professor Buckland (President of the Geological Society).

The President and Vice-President of the College of Surgeons.

The Master and Wardens of the Society of Apothecaries,

&c. &c. &c.

Several letters of excuse were sent, couched in the most respectful terms to the College, and signifying the different reasons, for the most part causes of unavoidable public business, which prevented the writers being present at the ceremony. Among these were letters from

The Earl of Eldon (Lord Chancellor).

The Dukeof Bedford.

The Marquess Camden.

The Earl Bathurst (Secretary of State for the Colonies).

H

The Lord Grenville (Chancellor of the University of Oxford).
The Bishops of London, Bristol, Exeter, Winchester.
Right Hon. George Canning (Secretary of State for Foreign
     Affairs).
Lord Viscount Palmerston (Secretary at War).
The Earl of Harrowby (President of the Council).
The Earl Spencer, K.G.

"When the guests had taken their seats, the president, preceded by the beadle carrying the mace and followed by more than fifty fellows, walked in procession to the great room of the library where a raised seat had been prepared, before which on a table were placed the cushion, the book of statutes and the mace.

"On each side of the president the censors seated themselves in chairs; the elects of the College were placed on the right hand, and the fellows occupied the benches around which had been appropriated to them.

"The president (wearing the decoration of the royal Guelphic order, which the king had been pleased to confer upon him that morning) then delivered an eloquent Latin oration to an audience of upwards of three hundred persons.

"When this was concluded, they all adjourned to the dining-room below and were treated with a sumptuous collation. His Royal Highness the Duke of York was pleased to drink to the prosperity of the College; and afterwards all their royal highnesses rose and proposed the health of the president of the College."

This was the proudest moment in Sir Henry Halford's life, and he gave a graceful and practical proof of his feeling towards the College, and those of his colleagues who had been associated with him in bringing it about, by forwarding to the treasurer of the College, Dr. Turner, a draft on his banker for £300 to defray the expenses of the opening.   It was enclosed in the following letter :

" My dear Sir,—

          " After the noble exertions which the fellows have made to furnish the means of rebuilding the College, and after their generous acquiescence in an expensive scheme, calculated however, to open the new building with splendour and *éclat*, and which seems to have succeeded perfectly, I hope it may be taken in good part if I place at your disposal as treasurer, a draft intended to cover the expenses of the collation.

" I am gratified by this opportunity of expressing to you my deep sense of your indefatigable zeal, and of your successful industry in preparing everything for the late ceremony, and of assuring you how much reason I have seen to admire your prudence in the management of the pecuniary concerns of the College, since you have been its treasurer.   Pray believe me, my dear sir, with high esteem,

          " Your faithful friend and servant,

                    " Henry Halford.

" Curzon Street, *June* 30*th*, 1825."

Shortly after the opening of the new building, as soon indeed as its internal arrangements were completed, Sir Henry as president suggested that evening meetings should be held from time

to time at the College. And this with the two-
fold object of bringing together the different
branches of the medical profession, so as to
remove prejudices and substitute a better feeling
in their stead ; and further, of bringing into
association with the profession at the College
representatives of all that is noble, venerable,
distinguished and learned in general society, in
science, and in the other professions. The idea
was felicitous, and as the arrangements made for
these meetings were judicious, they soon became
popular, and for several years were very successful. They were held monthly for the first six
months of the year at nine o'clock in the evening
and ended at eleven o'clock. Tea and coffee
were provided. The president took the chair at
a table in the great library, without his gown or
any of the other insignia of his office, with the
registrar of the College on his right and
supported on both sides by such of the officers
and seniors of the College as might be present.
The papers were to be read by the registrar,
except those by the president, who was at liberty
to read his own, and Sir Henry Halford always
did so. The papers, it was felt, should be on
such subjects especially as are peculiarly adapted
to excite interest in a mixed audience of gentle-

men and scholars, and are capable of being illustrated by literature, the common bond of connection of all the liberal professions. The papers contributed by Sir Henry Halford, Dr. Heberden, Dr. Macmichael, and some other fellows of the College were essentially of this character. No debating or speaking on the papers was permitted, but they often supplied to the company a subject for much interesting conversation and interchange of opinion during the remainder of the evening.

Perhaps foremost in interest and in importance of the papers communicated to the College by Sir Henry Halford were those " On the Influence of some of the Diseases of the Body on the Mind ; " " On the Education and Conduct of a Physician ; " and " On the Καῦσος of Aretæus." The last of these met with marked commendation by those best qualified to judge of it. The Archbishop of Canterbury, Dr. Howley, writes as follows :

"LONDON, *September* 17*th*, 1830.

" MY DEAR SIR,

" I have read your observations on the passage of Aretæus describing the καῦσος with more than common pleasure. The justness of the remarks and the elegance and propriety of the language are equally striking ; and I cannot help thinking that a series of disquisitions on a similar plan, would tend much to the illustration and in many instances the advancement of medical science.

"Believe me, my dear Sir,

"Truly yours,

"W. CANTUAR."

And from the Bishop of London, Dr. Blomfield :

"LONDON HOUSE, *February* 10*th*, 1831.

"MY DEAR SIR HENRY,

"I return your disquisition on the καῦσος with many thanks for your kindness in having permitted me to profit by the perusal of a composition not unworthy of your eminence as a master of the healing art, or of your reputation as a scholar, nor, let me add, of the still more important character, which you are not ashamed of being known to bear, as a Christian.

"Believe me, my dear Sir Henry,

"Yours very truly,

"C. J. LONDON.

"Sir HENRY HALFORD, Bart."

Whilst of the volume of "Essays and Orations" in which these and several others are collected, there are, among many letters, the following from Lord Grenville, a most competent judge; and from a distinguished member of the judicial bench, Sir J. A. Park :

"DROPMORE, *May 13th*, 1831.

"MY DEAR SIR,

"I thank you heartily for the little volume which you have had the kindness to send me. Its contents were not new to me, but I have again admired with fresh delight your truly elegant and simple (or therefore truly classic) style, both in Latin and in our own language, so opposite to the laboured and affected modes of writing now so prevalent in both. With this style well accords the character of the sentiments which it is so appropriately employed to express.

  *   *   *   *   *

"Believe me, dear Sir,

"Your attached and faithful friend,

"GRENVILLE.

"Sir H. HALFORD, Bart."

"BEDFORD SQUARE, *May 20th*, 1831.

"MY DEAR SIR HENRY,

"Even at the hazard of incurring for a few days the charge of ingratitude for continued kindness and friendship, I have declined to acknowledge the receipt of your valuable present, till I should have an opportunity of perusing all your essays and orations. That opportunity has been afforded me, and most willingly have I seized it, to peruse every part of the precious little work. I do assure you, Sir Henry, I do not use the language of flattery, but I have been delighted, not only with the matter (of which of course I am not always competent to judge), but with the style, language and impressiveness with which every sentence tells. And what delights me most is, that in all your judicious advice to the younger members of your profession, you never forget the character of the moralist and Christian. In this respect you imitate *our* illustrious magistrate, Lord Kenyon, who adopted for his judicial motto the dictum of Horace, but using *moribus* in the Christian sense :

> " Quid leges sine moribus
> Vanæ proficiant."

Let me then be allowed to conclude, and I do most sincerely offer you my most sincere wishes in your own impressive words—only changing the epithet because it does not apply yet to you :

" Valeas itaque, eximie vir ! otioque literato, et doctorum hominum colloquiis, et vitæ tuæ anteactæ recordatione diu perfruaris ! insigne medicis exemplum relicturus, amplam dicendi materiem oratori.

" I am, dear Sir Henry, with deep respect,

" Your very faithful servant,

" J. A. PARK."

These evening meetings at the College, and especially those of them when the paper was supplied by the president, Sir Henry Halford, were numerously attended, and among the visitors were generally a considerable number of the highest and most distinguished personages of the time. Among such were H.R.H. the Duke of Sussex, the Duke of Wellington, the Primates of England and of Ireland, the Lords Chancellor Lyndhurst and Brougham, the Marquis of Lansdowne, Earl Grey, Sir Robert Peel, and many other Cabinet Ministers, many of the bishops, and most of the judges.

Much of the success of these meetings depended, it is certain, on Sir Henry Halford, who brought all the private interest he possessed, and it was exceptionally great, to bear upon them ; and with the effect of making the College known and appreciated by many of the best and noblest in the land. In these efforts he was warmly seconded by many of the fellows of the College. These evening meetings at the College ceased in 1838. They had continued for more than ten years and had answered the purpose for which they had been instituted.

About this period Sir Henry Halford encountered some unpopularity among the junior members of his profession and of the College of Physicians, by the desire he always manifested to retain the connection between Oxford and Cambridge—the

especial seats of classical education in this country
—and the College of Physicians; and by his
unwillingness, save in exceptional circumstances,
to admit to the highest order and fullest privileges
of the College, that is to the fellowship, any who
had not shared in all the advantages of an English
university education.

Sir Henry's experience in his own person, and
what he had seen in the most distinguished physicians of his time, such as Dr. Heberden, Sir
George Baker, Dr. Warren and others, had satisfied
him of the paramount importance to the forming
of a physician, of an English university training
such as it then was.   It implied an excellent discipline of the understanding, giving precision to
thought and language, inducing a habit of close
attention and a patient application of the mind;
and in all these respects was the most fitting preparation and discipline for special and particularly
for medical study.

It was too, the best, indeed the only way,
of enabling the physician to add that dignity
to his profession "which had raised it in
England pre-eminently above the consideration
which it obtained in any other country of
the world"; and had fitted the English physician for associating on no inferior or unequal

terms with the wisest, best and highest in the land.

To the like effect, but more fully wrote a distinguished contemporary and friend of Sir Henry Halford—Dr. P. M. Latham. " In England," says he, " there always have been among physicians, those who have been upon an equality of education with the noblest and most learned of the land.   They have mixed with them at our public schools and universities, they have contended with them in honourable rivalry; and their minds have taken a congenial character from the similar studies of their youth.   At length they have all separated to their several destinies for life.   Some to the senate, some to the bar, some to the church, some to physic.   These men so educated have ever afterwards looked with esteem upon each other, and each other's pursuits.   And thus have the most illustrious men of every age, who could know nothing of physic as a profession, viewing it through those whom they have known engaged in it, been compelled to regard it with reverence and honour.   In this way a credit has been derived to our common profession, in which every individual in every rank of it, has partaken, when those whose good opinion is most coveted, have taken their estimate of physic and physicians from contemplating the characters of such men as Dr. Heberden and Sir George Baker." *

Sir Henry Halford equally with Dr. Latham desired to have physicians still instituted in the same discipline and still reared in fellowship and communion with the wisest and best men ; and that, not for the sake of what is ornamental merely and becoming to their character, but because he was persuaded that that discipline which renders the mind most capacious of wisdom and most capacious of virtue, can hold the torch and light the path to the sublimest discoveries in every science.   It was the same discipline which contributed to form the mind of Newton and of Locke, of Harvey and of Sydenham.†

The English physician indeed, at the period to

* "Lectures on subjects connected with Clinical Medicine," by P. M. Latham, M.D.   London, 1836, p. 28.

† "Notwithstanding the repressive influence of mediæval statutes and the want of any organised system of medical instruction, the medical students of the English universities very generally attained the highest rank amongst the physicians of the metropolis and elsewhere.   They entered the profession generally late in life, but with all the advantages of the classical, as well as medical education, and were thus associated more intimately in rank and estimation with the higher classes of society, than those, whose early studies had been of a less refined and general character ; and there are many reasons which should induce us to conclude that the high social

which I refer, had come to be considered as combining in his person, not only the qualifications necessary for the successful practice of physic, but those which give dignity to his professional, and respectability to his private character. He was distinguished by large attainments as a scholar, by sound religious principles as a Christian ; by practical worth and virtue as a good member of society, and by polished manners as a well-bred gentleman.*

position which physicians have hitherto been enabled to maintain in this country—so different from that which they occupy on the continent of Europe—is not a little owing to this admixture of well-educated gentlemen, so many of whom have been supplied by the English universities. The privileges also which were accorded to the College of Physicians, though long stigmatised as unjust and illiberal, and the cause of frequent litigation, especially about the period of which we are now speaking, had a similar tendency; and it may be reasonably doubted, now that these privileges are to a great extent abandoned, whether the medical profession will long be able to maintain, as hitherto, the same estimation in society with the members of the professions of the church and the law." (Life of Thomas Young, M.D., F.R.S., by George Peacock, D.D., Dean of Ely, &c. 8vo. London, 1855, p. 121.)

* *Gentleman's Magazine*, March, 1834, p. 334. Instances were no doubt to be found then, as at all other periods, in which some of these characteristics were wanting, but then the deficiencies were always felt and perceived, censured and regretted, not simply by reason of the deformity thereby brought upon the character and conduct of the individual, but because they were departures from an established usage, violations of a general rule, and disappointments of a well-grounded expectation.

But a number of the junior fellows of the College of Physicians thought otherwise than their president. They contended that the higher order and offices of the College should be open to all, no matter where or how educated, provided they came up to a standard of *mere medical knowledge*. By perseverance and pertinacity they at length won over a majority of the fellows and succeeded in 1835 in severing the time-honoured connection of the College of Physicians with the two universities, and in altering the whole constitution of their institution.

Opposed as all this was to the convictions and wishes of Sir Henry Halford, he nevertheless in his office of president, continued strictly loyal to the College as represented by the majority, and carried out honestly, with prudence and judgment, the various important alterations which were then introduced.

Those who remember the physicians of the period of which I am writing—and there are a few still living who do so, myself among that number—their classical culture, their staid philosophic habit of mind, their social position, and the estimation in which their College was then held by the best and highest of the land, can but lament the change in all these respects which has since taken place, in sequel to, and as it would seem partly in consequence of the changes of 1835. While the other branches of the medical profession—the surgeons and the apothecaries—have improved their culture and position, the physicians have lost much of that which they formerly possessed, and have reached a level, there is no denying it, not equal to that which they once enjoyed in this country.

It was said not long since in one of our leading reviews,* and I cannot gainsay the truth of the statement, that "no one comparing the present race of physicians with those of a time not so very remote, can fail to observe a remarkable dissimilarity, less from a strictly professional point of view, than from the difference in their mental equipment. The older physicians were usually the foremost representatives of the best and widest culture of their time. At once scholars and men of science, they commanded respect not more by the vastness of their erudition than, it must be confessed, by the results of their practical skill. They were often distinguished in literature. Arbuthnot and Garth could associate with the wits of their day without any sense of inferiority as regards culture. Our latter-day doctors

* *Fortnightly Review*, June 1885, p. 780.

have altogether lapsed from the category of scholars ; they are now probably the least learned of the three liberal professions. Even as men of science we are no longer up to the level of our predecessors."

Sir George Tuthill, a distinguished physician and one of the leading fellows of the College, had undertaken to deliver the Harveian oration in June, 1835, but he was cut off, after a short illness by acute inflammation of the larynx, early in the month of April. Lest the anniversary oration should be wanting, Sir Henry Halford undertook to supply the place of his friend, and did so on the 25th June before a large and highly distinguished audience, in an excellent address of choice Latin, which met the approval of all his colleagues, and was acknowledged in the College annals as follows :

" *Junii, Die* xxv, 1835.—On this our great anniversary, the College cannot separate, without expressing its grateful sense of the many obligations it owes to its president. On the lamented death of Sir George Tuthill, who was the Harveian orator designated for this year, the president undertook in a comparatively short space of time to supply his place. And when it is considered that this is the third occasion upon which Sir

Henry Halford has performed this arduous duty, the College wishes to record how much it feels indebted to him for the zeal, ability and eloquence with which he has discharged the functions of its public orator."

The following letter from Dr. Gordon, is one among many congratulating the orator on his success :

" My dear Sir Henry,

"Will you permit a very humble, but at the same time a very sincere and grateful friend, to add his congratulations to the many you have this day received on the delivery of the Harveian oration, and to assure you on the faith of a calm and unprejudiced observer, that its reception was in all respects such as could be desired by those to whom your honour and reputation are dear.

"I sat by Lockhart—the calm but heightened glow of pleasure which beamed in his countenance at some of the more striking passages ; the honest fervour of Sir Robert Inglis, who told me that he did not know there was such Latin to be found in modern times, are perhaps more touching testimonials, but not more gratifying than the *general* approbation with which your discourse was received by men of all parties. To my mind, one of the chief beauties of the oration was its dignified

and graceful simplicity ; and the effect was greatly
heightened by the eloquent manner in which you
delivered it.   I was at the very extremity of the
room and every syllable—every inflexion of the
voice—came to me as distinctly as if uttered in a
small room.   There appeared to me but one
feeling, one sentiment on the matter.
　　" Believe me to be, my dear Sir Henry,
　　　"Your grateful friend and servant,
　　　　　　　" JAMES A. GORDON.

" 2 FINSBURY SQUARE, *June* 25*th*."

From this time until Sir Henry was disabled by
the illness which terminated his life, he continued
to perform with regularity and assiduity all the
duties of his high office at the College.   Among
the most important and delicate of these, was the
selection to the fellowship speciali gratiâ, from
among such physicians of the College as had not
been educated at Oxford or Cambridge.   The
names of Sir James McGrigor, Bart., Dr. William
Babington, Sir Henry Holland, Bart., Dr. Prout,
Dr. Roget, Dr. Bright, and Dr. Wilson-Philip,
who were admitted fellows on the individual
nomination of Sir Henry Halford, are a sufficient
proof of his care and wisdom in the selection.

It is but just to add here that Sir Henry was
always ready to waive his individual rights and

privileges as president of the College, in deference to the expressed or even the presumed views of the fellows. There are numerous instances of this recorded in the Annals of the College, all of them showing how solicitous he was to maintain peace and avoid the semblance of offence to his colleagues.

For the rest, his duties at the College were for the most part of a routine and uninteresting character, and may be passed over by his biographer. There was nothing at this period of sufficient public or special interest in the proceedings of the College of Physicians to call for remark in a life of Sir Henry Halford.

Sir Henry's love of his profession and his devotion to the College of Physicians continued to the last. In the latest of his essays read to the College, that "On some Results of the successful Practice of Physic," he says : "Let me add, in evidence of the sincerity with which I have represented the frequent occasions of the purest mental gratification which the physician finds in the exercise of his calling, independently of any other consideration, and contrary to the maxim in Horace,

> Nemo, quam sibi sortem
> Seu ratio dederit seu fors objecerit, illâ
> Contentus vivat? Laudet diversa sequentes?

that if I were to begin my life again I would adopt the profession of physic." And "amongst these gratifications, I should be ungrateful to you, if I did not enumerate the repeated pleasure of meeting and co-operating with you for the improvement of medicine, and for the promotion of the respectability of our profession, in these evening assemblies at the College; and when it shall please the great Creator to remove me to another world, which must necessarily be at no very distant day, some of you who now listen to me may bear in mind these my unfeigned sentiments and attachment to our common profession, and not be surprised if you should hear that

Occidit, et dulces moriens reminiscitur Argos."

In 1843 Sir Henry Halford's health began to break. He was at the College for the last time the 27th of September, 1843, when he presided at a meeting of the elects—a class in the College that no longer exists. He died, as has been stated, the 9th of March, 1844. On his death-bed, he had expressed to Dr. Turner, the treasurer of the College, and to other of the senior fellows, his conviction that Dr. Paris was best fitted of all the fellows to succeed him in the office of president; and on the morrow of Palm Sunday, 1844, "postridie Palmarum," Dr. John Ayrton Paris was elected to that office.

At a committee of the College held on that day, the following resolution was passed unanimously :

" In order more effectually to perpetuate the distinguished services rendered to the College by their late president, Sir Henry Halford (extending through a period of twenty-five years), as well as to mark the admiration and gratitude with which they have been regarded by his contemporaries ; it was unanimously resolved that these sentiments should be recorded in the Annals of the College, *and embodied in a suitable inscription on a tablet to be placed in the library.*"

I add, I do so not without a blush, that no such tablet has been put up, and that the library has been and still is conspicuous for its absence.

It may be, it was thought on further consideration, though there is nothing in the Annals or other documents of the College to bear out the supposition, that no inscription was really needed, and that the edifice itself was the best memorial of him, to whom its existence was mainly due. Such was evidently the opinion of the Harveian orator of 1848—Dr. Francis Hawkins—who, in reference to Sir Henry Halford, expressed himself as follows :

"Ardebat, mihi credite, singulari quodam amore in hoc Collegium, cui tam diu, omnium consessu, præfuit. Quid enim ? testabor has ipsas ædes ? quas, maximis curis et laboribus suis, nobis adparavit ; quas dedicavit oratione purâ sic, ut Latine loqui pœne solus videretur ; quas igitur ei, quem prope dixerim conditorem nostrum quintum, perpetuo fore monumento prorsus existimo. Hic, hic inquam, si quærat quispiam *Halfordi* monumentum, circumspiciat."

CHAPTER VII

So early in Sir Henry Halford's medical career as 1793, when he was not yet twenty-seven years of age, he had been honoured with the appointment of physician-extraordinary to the king. Yet strange to say, nothing can now be recalled of the circumstances—though they must have been very exceptional—which led to that appointment.

In 1801 he was called into medical attendance on the Duchess of Gloucester, and shortly afterwards on H.R.H. the Duke of Gloucester, a brother of George III.; and he continued to attend the duke up to his death in 1805, as he did the Duchess of Gloucester to her death in 1807.

The first of the family of George III. by whom he was consulted was the Duke of Kent in the early part of 1802, who continued to consult him at intervals up to his marriage.   The duke

enjoyed exceptionally good health and had little
need of physic or physicians. His dislike of
medicine was so strong that he could be induced
to take it only on extreme occasions. His last
illness at Sidmouth in 1820, was thought to have
had a fatal issue from his refusal to take the dose
prescribed for him at the very commencement of
the attack by his domestic physician, Dr. Wilson.

Of the Duke of Kent's kindly feeling for Sir
Henry Halford, the following letter is a proof :

"THE LODGE, CASTLE HILL,
" *Wednesday morning, September 1st,* 1813.

" MY DEAR SIR HENRY,

" Having at length been able to find a
horse to replace your little favourite, I lost not
a moment in sending him to you, but hope you
will confer on me the obligation of *accepting* him
from me as a keepsake, and as a mark of my
grateful acknowledgment for your kind and
friendly attention to me upon the occasion of
my late severe accident, of which I shall ever
entertain a lively recollection. The only condition I entreat permission to make, is that if
ever you should get tired of him you will then
send him back to me. You are aware he has
never to my knowledge been rode by a lady;
and therefore, if you mean him for your daughter,
he should be put under the tuition of Fozard of
Park Lane before she is trusted to mount him.

He has no vice, is perhaps at times a little shy of odd objects, but perfectly tractable if used kindly.

"I have long wished for an opportunity of expressing to you how deeply I feel your unremitting attention to that dear little angel, my younger sister, who I may say to you is one of the greatest comforts of my life, and I hope you will consider this trifling gift as a small mark also of my eternal gratitude for your care of dearest Sophy, whose life to me is of more value than any language can express.

"You will I know hear with pleasure that nothing is wanting to complete my recovery from my late accident but the wound closing in my left arm, which there is every hope another week will accomplish, and then, when I can once get on horseback, I shall soon recover my strength, which, at present, certainly is not what it was. As, if I recollect right, this is your Windsor day, may I beg of you to give my kindest love to all my sisters, and to lay my duty at the queen's feet, adding that if by this day week I am able to do without bandages or dressings I shall certainly be at Windsor, but if disappointed in that, I am sure all will approve of my postponing it.

" It only now remains for me to assure you of the unutterable sentiments of friendship and esteem with which I ever am,

"My dear Sir Henry,

"Yours most faithfully,

"EDWARD."

In the following year—1803—Sir Henry was consulted by the Duke of Cumberland, whose entire confidence and "sincere friendship" he soon succeeded in obtaining; and who from this time trusted the care of his own health, and when he married in 1815, that of his duchess, wholly to Sir Henry, up to the time, 1837, when the duke succeeded to the crown of Hanover, and left England.

Towards the end of 1809, Sir Henry was sent for, in conjunction with Dr. Baillie, to attend the Princess Amelia, the youngest and favourite daughter of George III. The princess resided with her sister the Princess Mary, afterwards Duchess of Gloucester, in a house at Windsor— Augusta Lodge—in proximity to the castle. She had then been ill for some time and attended by Sir Francis Milman, Dr. Saunders, Dr. Heberden, and a local practitioner named Pope. Her complaint was consumption of the lungs, a disease for which medicine *then* could effect but little, and in the symptoms and progress of which the princess herself perceived but little if any amendment. With an anxiety, natural under such circumstances, she felt a desire for an entire change in her medical attendants. Sir Henry Halford and

Dr. Baillie were at her own request substituted in place of her former physicians, and they had the entire medical care of her Royal Highness up to her death.

Sir Henry and Dr. Baillie were entirely agreed in their view of the case, and drew up two joint reports—one, containing a full and most candid statement to be submitted to the king ; the other, which the princess herself was to be allowed to see, modified in such manner as to avoid any ill consequences to her feelings and maintain that hope in her mind, without which, such chance as there might be of recovery, would be extinguished.

But the princess's bodily malady was not all she had to suffer. She had private mental trials and troubles of no ordinary character, consequent upon the secret marriage she had contracted with General Fitzroy. These rendered her medical treatment all the more difficult, and the office of her physicians the more delicate, particularly in the latter period of her illness. It was so especially in the case of Sir Henry Halford, whose warm sympathy with his patient had secured her entire confidence, and made him the involuntary depository of all her troubles and wishes. She desired Sir Henry to become the medium of communication between herself and the king. He was thus placed in a very embarrassing situation. He felt that it would be altogether foreign to his position and an act of great presumption to undertake such an office. It seems too, that it would have been attended with peculiar responsibility on account of the king's state of mind, at that time verging again upon insanity. Any such step too, was earnestly deprecated by the Princess Amelia's most affectionate sister, the Princess Mary. To Sir Henry's great distress on account of the disappointment inflicted on the princess, he was compelled, in the best way he could, to decline compliance with her request.

During Sir Henry Halford's attendance on the Princess Amelia, he had frequent interviews with the king, and was soon honoured by his Majesty's entire confidence. One of the king's latest hours of rational life was employed in dictating a letter to the Princess Amelia, which he directed in Sir Henry Halford's presence and committed to his charge, to express his satisfaction that she had received the holy Sacrament that morning, and had sought for comfort under her sufferings, where only it could be found — in religion.

The princess died two days afterwards, and to

Sir Henry Halford was assigned the office of communicating the sad intelligence to the king. The king, whose mind was even then giving way, had always looked upon the previous visitations of this dreadful calamity as trials of his faith and obedience, and Sir Henry in his interview with the king, took an opportunity to say he was going to try his Majesty's piety. The king immediately answered he knew what he meant, and that the Princess Amelia he supposed was dead. Sir Henry replied it was so, upon which the king went off in a low rambling way, which lasted some time, when he became more composed, and mentioned her again, saying : " Poor girl." *

Shortly after this, Sir Henry Halford was called upon to make a further communication, and this of a very delicate character, to the king. Every day questions were expected from his Majesty as to the disposition of the Princess Amelia's property, her will, &c. ; and the bequest by her of everything she possessed to General Fitzroy, was a delicate subject to touch upon. " The Queen dared not; Perceval and the Chancellor successively undertook the disclosure and shrunk from it, imposing it on Sir Henry.

* " Memoir of Plumer Ward," by Edmund Phipps, vol. i. p. 298.

Never, he says, can he forget the feelings with which, having requested some private conversation with the king, after the other physicians were gone, he was called into a window with the light falling so full on his countenance, that even the poor, nearly blind king could see it. He asked whether it would be agreeable to him to hear how the Princess Amelia had disposed of her little property. "Certainly, certainly, I want to know," with great eagerness. Sir Henry reminded him that at the beginning of his illness *he* had appointed Fitzroy to ride with her; how he had left him with her at Weymouth; how it was natural and proper she should leave him some token for these services; that excepting jewels she had nothing to leave, and had bequeathed them all to him: that the Prince of Wales, thinking jewels a very inappropriate bequest for a man, had given Fitzroy a pecuniary compensation for them; and had distributed slight tokens to all the attendants and friends of the princess, giving the bulk of the jewels to the Princess Mary, her most constant and kindest of nurses. Upon this, the poor king exclaimed, "Quite right, just like the Prince of Wales;" and no more was said.*

* "Diaries of a Lady of Quality from 1797 to 1844." Edited with notes by A. Haywood, Esq., Q.C. London, 1864, p. 214.

In the course of one of the many interviews, which Sir Henry had with George III. during his attendance on the Princess Amelia, the king charged him, in the event of his Majesty experiencing a return of his mental derangement, that he—Sir Henry Halford—should at once take upon himself the medical care of Him, adding that Sir Henry must promise not to leave him ; and that if he needed help he should call in Dr. Heberden, and in case of yet further need which would necessarily occur, if Parliament took up the matter, Dr. Baillie. Further, the king made Sir Henry promise that he should never be left entirely alone with any medical person specially engaged in the department of insanity. (Letter of the queen to Mr. Perceval without date.)

On the illness of the king which occurred almost immediately after the death of the Princess Amelia, Sir Henry Halford was summoned to attend, and his prompt introduction of Dr. Heberden and Dr. Baillie, at once ensured the confidence of the queen and other members of the royal family. But Sir Henry soon became aware that all the acts of himself and of his medical colleagues were closely but secretly watched on the part of the Prince of Wales, by persons on the spot. Anxious to stop this espionage, Sir Henry went direct to the prince and gave him the most detailed and most accurate statement of the situation of the king.   The prince expressed his gratitude, not unmixed with surprise, at his candour.   Sir Henry promised that henceforth the prince might depend upon always having from him the most accurate information, if he would only promise not to seek it from any other sources.   The prince gave the promise and kept it.

These reports to the Prince of Wales, during the earlier portion of the king's illness and while there seemed to be a prospect of recovery, were made once a week or oftener, and either orally or by letter.   The following letter, one among many of the like character before me, will give some idea of the scope and character of Sir Henry's report to the prince :

"Sir,

"I find that the whole of the last week has been passed by his Majesty in a more tranquil and composed manner than any of the last three weeks. As this has been occasioned so obviously by the greater degree of restraint under which the king has lived, it does not admit of our inferring with any propriety or safety that his Majesty's malady has declined proportionally : but we are justified in flattering ourselves that the exclusion from all occasions of excitement, and a system of steady, prudent control may lead to that improvement which we are all so anxious to witness. Some reference has been noticed to his Majesty's favourite errors, but not in any considerable degree and not frequently.

"I am, Sir, with the highest respect,

"Your Royal Highness's faithful servant,

"HENRY HALFORD.

"*June 8th*, 1811."

Sir Henry, after his interview with the Prince of Wales went to the queen and told her what he had done. "She with a tremendous frown expressed great astonishment. Sir Henry stated the obvious reason for the step he had taken; she paused, her brow cleared: "You are quite right, sir; it is proper that the Prince of Wales should be informed." *   From that moment it is said, confidence and intimacy were renewed between the queen and the prince. And such progress did Sir Henry make in the favour of the Prince of Wales, that in September, 1810, he was appointed physician to his Royal Highness, who further secured for him in 1812, on the first vacancy that occurred, the appointment of physician-in-ordinary to the king.

* "Diaries of a Lady of Quality from 1797 to 1844."

K

In their medical attendance on George III., Sir Henry Halford, Dr. Baillie and Dr. Heberden were associated with the two brothers, Dr. John and Dr. Robert Willis.*   That there was a difference of opinion among the physicians as to the treatment of their august patient was notorious. Sir Henry Halford and Dr. Baillie, both of them in the first rank of the medical profession and physicians of the highest reputation, and Dr. Heberden generally in accord with them, felt a common sense of difficulty, on account of the undue and as they thought injurious authority, which by the council of great officers appointed to assist the queen, was allowed to the Willises, under the idea of their special and exceptional experience in the care of the insane.   The Willises were established at Windsor in the suite of apartments occupied by the king and his attendants, and were one or other of them in daily, almost hourly, attendance on his Majesty.

At that time, the principle had not been established as it has since been in this country by Conolly and his followers, of the necessity of kindness in the treatment of persons whose reason was in abeyance.   The Willises were in favour of the opposite and older method—that of severity

* "Annual Register" of 1816.   Chronicle, p. 2.

and, if need be, of force and physical restraint. Letters at Wistow contain evidence, supported by Mr. Battiscomb, a respectable apothecary at Windsor, of the very unbecoming violence employed upon the king in a former attack and in the presence of the elder Willis, by a person in his employ. Such treatment of the king was repugnant alike to the feelings and the professional judgment of Sir Henry and Dr. Baillie, as it was also to those relatives of the royal sufferer who were cognisant of it ; but they were powerless under the circumstances wholly to prevent it. They succeeded however, up to a certain point, as the following letters go to show. The first is the rough draft in Sir Henry Halford's writing, of a letter, without date or signature, to the Duke of York, to which the second is the reply :

" SIR,

"On my return to Windsor yesterday I found the king's countenance expressing some remains of that eagerness and excitement which have prevailed in his Majesty's manner throughout the week. The queen's visit however, was a satisfactory one, and there was nothing in the king's manner or conversation with the physicians in the evening but what was dignified and proper. His Majesty has slept nearly six hours in the course of the night, but has manifested some nervousness by the adjustment of his bed-clothes this morning, and we find him more talkative, more excited than is well, in our interview. I understand that there was a palpable reference to the familiar delusion yesterday.

" The irritability and eagerness to which I have alluded above may be accounted for, satisfactorily perhaps, by referring them to *the new circumstances in which the king was placed last week by the admission of his Majesty to a greater indulgence*, and I assure your Royal Highness that they ought not to detract a mite from the opinion which we have uniformly maintained of the king's ultimate recovery."

To this the Duke of York replies as follows :

"STABLE YARD, 31*st October*, 1810.

" DEAR SIR,

" I am most truly sensible of your kind attention in relieving my anxiety by informing me yourself of the real state of our beloved king.

" It is a great comfort to me to learn that you are so thoroughly satisfied with the system of management which you from the first proposed for his Majesty's present indisposition. It is certainly the most congenial to my feelings, and I trust by keeping up the confidence which he has placed in you, that it will cause a prompter and more certain cure than any other means, the very thought of which I confess for every reason makes one shudder, and which nothing but the most urgent necessity could warrant.

" I am happy to learn that his Majesty had some comfortable sleep yesterday afternoon, and am willing to flatter myself that it is a proof that the present attack is less violent than any former one, and that we may therefore look forward with certainty to a much speedier recovery.

"I shall be at Windsor without fail to-morrow by two o'clock in the afternoon, and will call at Augusta Lodge before dinner in the hope of being able to see you for a moment.

" Believe me ever, dear Sir,

" Yours most sincerely.

" FREDERICK.

"Sir HENRY HALFORD, Bart."

During the first period of the king's illness the attendances of Sir Henry Halford and Dr. Baillie from London were frequent and prolonged. It would seem that nearly half of the year 1811 was passed by Sir Henry at Windsor, and doubtless as long by his colleague, Dr. Baillie. At first great hopes were entertained by all the physicians in attendance of the king's speedy and entire recovery, but these were doomed to disappointment. By the month of October, 1811, recovery was deemed to be very improbable, and by the following March all idea of it had to be given up.* From about this period a visit once a week and separately by Sir Henry Halford, Dr. Baillie and Dr. Heberden, was considered to meet all the requirements of the case. Sir Henry attended on the king at Windsor regularly on Thursdays, going down in the morning and returning sometimes the same day, but oftener on the following morning.

Sir Henry was in close attendance upon the king towards the last, and with his colleagues, Dr. Baillie, Dr. Heberden, Dr. Robert Willis, and Sir David Dundas, was present at his death on the 29th January, 1820.

Sir Henry was consulted by Queen Charlotte for the first time in the spring of 1815, and his services on that occasion were fully appreciated by her Majesty and were graciously acknowledged by a handsome present of plate and the following letter :

"The Queen being perfectly aware of her inadequacy to recompense the attention she received from Sir Henry Halford during her illness, she takes this method of returning him

---

* "Lord Colchester's Diary," vol. ii. pp. 344, 373.

thanks for it, and begs he will accept the box which accompanies this as a mark of her regard.

"CHARLOTTE.

"WINDSOR CASTLE, *the 27th August* 1815."

He continued to attend the queen at intervals, and in November, 1817, advised her Majesty to repair to Bath and try the waters there. In January, 1818, Sir Henry addressed to the Prince Regent the following letter :

"WINDSOR CASTLE, *January 23rd*, 1818.

"SIR,

"As the Queen has not been quite well within the last few days, I have the confidence to flatter myself that your Royal Highness would desire to receive a letter from me containing an authentic account of her Majesty's indisposition.

"Her Majesty's symptoms do not differ in their nature nor much in the degree at which they prevail at present, from what I have observed them now for some months past : the principal one is a distressing shortness of breath, not a difficulty of breathing, on any exertion, and this recurs sometimes with so much severity as to appear to justify an apprehension that if the effort in which her Majesty be at the moment engaged were carried further or persevered in, it would be more than her nature could sustain. In these circumstances a contraction takes place in the muscle which separates the chest from the bas ventre, by which the organs of respiration are greatly embarrassed; and it appears constantly that the condition of the stomach, if weakened by any accidental cause, is one great source from whence this disposition to spasm arises. It is there that our remedies are applicable with most effect, and this was the principal ground on which I humbly recommended it to her Majesty to repair to Bath.

"On the whole I would not say that her Majesty's indisposition has become more urgent of late, but that her powers of constitution to resist it were more obviously diminished; and this must be expected to be the case as her Majesty advances further in age. The symptoms, I dare venture to assure your Royal Highness, will admit of palliation, but they are beyond our art to remove entirely. Her Majesty seems sometimes to take alarm about herself I think, and it is palpable that anything which affects the feelings disposes her more to a seizure of the disorder. Your Royal Highness's good nature will easily therefore permit me to entreat, that you will not take notice of this letter in any communication to Windsor, nor appear to know that her Majesty has complained more of late, than the period of her life and the season of the year, and the sad tale of late events, so affecting to your Royal Highness's own health and peace of mind, may well account for.

" I only add further that I am, Sir, with affectionate respect and attachment,

"Your Royal Highness's faithful servant,

"HENRY HALFORD."

Some days later Sir Henry wrote to the Prince Regent as follows :

" SIR,

"If I had had the honour of writing to your Royal Highness yesterday, I should have had the happiness of stating that the hopes I had held out to your Royal Highness of being able to mitigate her Majesty's symptoms had been well confirmed by the effect of the queen's medicines, and that her Majesty was certainly better. In fact, the queen had passed Monday, Tuesday and Wednesday with much less complaint, but yesterday morning a communication was made to her Majesty which affected her feelings very much and distressed her exceedingly. In fact, her Majesty could not dine with the Royal Family, and she passed the whole day in tears ; nor did her Majesty sleep last night, but I have the satisfaction of hearing that her Majesty had had a little sleep this morning.

" What the ultimate effect of this discomfiture to her Majesty's feelings may be on her disorder I cannot speak with confidence, but your Royal Highness is well aware that any depression of the powers of the frame, however temporary, in a malady where all the energies of the system are required to support itself under its attacks, must be of some ill consequence. I will hope, however, that time and affectionate attention may weaken the impression gradually, but I must acknowledge to your Royal Highness, with the same candour and sincerity with which I stated my opinion of her Majesty's symptoms in my last letter, that amongst the causes which I should find most reason to lament in the progress of her Majesty's treatment as likely to obviate and thwart its effect, I dreaded none so much as anxiety of mind.

"I need not assure your Royal Highness of my most respectful affectionate interest in all that concerns her Majesty's comfort and recovery. In contributing to her Majesty's ease, if I can do so, I know I contribute to your Royal Highness's happiness, and nothing gratifies me so much as being, sir, an useful as well as a most attached faithful servant.

"HENRY HALFORD."

In May Sir Francis Milman, the physician-in-ordinary to the queen, was joined with Sir Henry Halford in attendance on her Majesty, and they continued to attend the queen to her death. The queen's malady had issued in dropsy—an accumulation of water in her limbs and in her chest, which after a time no medicines materially relieved. In September Sir Henry, in reply to a searching question from the queen, communicated to her Majesty his fears as to the issue of her illness. The following account of that interview is endorsed by Sir Henry Halford : " A passage in the queen's illness shortly before she died."

"SUNDAY, *September* 13*th*, 1818.

" The Queen sent for me at 8½ yesterday evening and almost immediately said ' I have determined, sir, the first time I saw you alone to ask you whether you do not really think that my constitution is giving way.' So serious a question, madame, demands a sincere answer; and I must own to your Majesty that though there be no vital organ diseased perhaps in your Majesty's system, the whole frame is acting so irregularly as to make me doubt whether it be equal to bear the weight of your complaint. After a pause, her Majesty continued, ' I have sometimes thought it would do, and then it has appeared as if it would not. Your medicines have all produced their effect, but they go to a certain point and no further. Is there not something nervous in my complaint?'

" The symptoms which are so distressing to your Majesty are of a nervous nature, but they are peculiar to an affection of the vital organs, and your Majesty must feel that a malady there, is most important. May I humbly ask your Majesty if there be any anxiety of mind which gives your disease an advantage over you. 'No, sir, no. I feel extremely anxious to get back to Windsor. I was gaining strength, but I have lost it again, and am weaker to-day than ever. I have never recovered the attack of a fortnight since.'

"With regard to your Majesty's strength, as your digestive organs are in a good state, it is reasonable to expect that that may be restored. 'Well, sir, that is a good thing at least, is it not?' 'Yes, madame.'

"An hour after this Miss Rice, one of her Majesty's attendants, came out of the room, overcome in her feelings and in tears. She had been so affected by her Majesty's countenance and manner, which were those of a person occupied in devotion and prayer.

"When I went to wish her Majesty a good night at half-past ten, I found her very composed, and in the most gracious kind way she thanked me for my attention to her. Her Majesty had rather a better night than usual.

"HENRY HALFORD."

Early in November, Sir Henry wrote to the Prince Regent as follows:

"SIR,

"There is a little refreshment of the frame within the last thirty hours, but there is no real amendment. The disease has not advanced *sensibly* perhaps, but without doubt it is making a silent progress and the issue of it ultimately cannot be a doubtful one. In this state of circumstances, I dare say, your Royal Highness will in your affection and prudence decide not to go to a distance. I humbly presume to say, pray do not, for I assure your Royal Highness that Sir Francis Milman and myself are both decidedly of opinion that we cannot depend upon her Majesty's continuance amongst us the time it would be necessary for your Royal Highness's journey merely to Ragley and back."

The queen after much suffering, which she bore with great fortitude and resignation, expired on the 17th of November, 1818.

The Duke of York consulted Sir Henry Halford for the first time in 1803, his duchess somewhat later, and they both continued to avail themselves of his medical services as long as they lived. The Duchess of York after a long and painful illness, in which she was attended by Sir Henry Halford, died, somewhat suddenly at the last, at Oatlands on the 6th of August, 1820. The Duke of York, who had been often an invalid and in need of Sir Henry's professiona aid, gave the first indications of serious indisposition early in the month of June, 1826. But for some time before that a difficulty in ascending stairs or in assuming a recumbent posture in bed had been remarked. So much indeed was the difficulty of breathing aggravated by lying down that the duke passed his nights frequently in an armchair. On the duke's return from Ascot races the signs of a dropsical disposition became decided in a diminished secretion of urine, the presence of thirst, and swelling of the feet and ankles. His Royal Highness went to Brighton on the 14th of August for the benefit of change of air. Sir Henry Halford and Dr. Macmichael, his physicians, accompanied him ; and it is to Dr. Macmichael's " Account " of the duke's illness that I am indebted for the following particulars of its progress.

It was at Brighton that, the swelling of the lower extremities increasing, the first symptom exhibited itself, which induced the physicians to speak with distrust and alarm of the final issue of the illness. From the extremely distended skin an oozing of serous fluid took place which, though trifling in appearance to a casual observer, yet could not be seen without anxiety by those who are aware how prone a limb, under such circumstances, is to put on a gangrenous state, as the vital powers gradually yield and the constitution is reduced to a feeble condition.

It was at this period that a difficult question arose. Early in the duke's illness, Sir Herbert Taylor, a most confidential friend of his Royal Highness, had promised in consequence of the urgent importunity of his royal master to announce to him the first approach of danger, so that he might not be taken by surprise on such an occasion. The prognosis which the physicians in attendance were now obliged to form of the ultimate event of the case was, in consequence of the symptoms above mentioned, now become much more unfavourable. The question therefore arose whether this was to be then told to the patient, and it led to the following correspondence :

"Sir HERBERT TAYLOR to Sir HENRY HALFORD.

[PRIVATE.] "HORSE GUARDS, *August* 18*th*, 1826.

" MY DEAR SIR HENRY,

"I am going to Brighton to-morrow afternoon to see H.R.H. upon some points of business, and I am naturally anxious before I go to learn from you what is at this period and since your last visit, your opinion of H.R.H.'s case, and whether his situation is such as to call for the performance of the solemn pledge you know that I entered into before H.R.H. left Audley Square, and which I consider it to be my sacred duty to perform.   H.R.H.'s words were, ' I must not be taken by surprise nor treated like a child.   I must be told in *due time* what I have to expect, and I depend upon you for the disclosure as soon as you find that there is any apprehension of danger.'   I gave the promise.   H.R.H. asured me it put him at his ease, and before he left Brompton Park he reminded me of *my duty*.

" May I at once tell him that your opinion respecting his situation is not so favourable as it was, if he should press me with questions; that it is one of danger, though not without hope ?

" Believe me ever,

" Most truly yours,

" C. H. TAYLOR."

Sir Henry replied as follows:

" KING'S LODGE, WINDSOR PARK,
August 18th, midnight.

" MY DEAR TAYLOR,

" The time is not yet arrived, nor do I know, considering the nature of my illustrious patient's disease, when it may arrive, that I shall consider it admissible to let the Duke of York into a knowledge of the danger of it.

" There are some maladies in which we find the hopes of our patients predominate to so unreasonable a degree as to render it expedient on many accounts to repress those hopes; but if we cannot keep up and maintain the confidence of a sick

man under a visitation of the duke's particular
disease, his despondency destroys him prematurely,
and all the efforts of our art are puny, inadequate,
useless.

" I must entreat you therefore, my dear Taylor,
to refer his Royal Highness to me for any explanation of his difficulties.   You know my opinion of
your good sense, of your good heart, and of your
attachment to your excellent master ; but this is
my especial province, and whatever you may feel
of apprehension, I entreat you to hide it all within
your own bosom, and to parry every form of
solicitation, every appeal to your integrity, every
demand upon your attachment, by an absolute
reference to my *judgment*, to my affectionate
interest in H.R.H.'s comfort and recovery, and
to *my duty*.   I shall be ready with my answer
whenever his Royal Highness be pleased to
appeal to me, but in the peculiar circumstances of
his case it will be well if my practised discretion
be equal to all the niceties which the formidable
distemper and the *character of the duke's mind*
throw around the management of it.

" I have not answered your question without
laying before the king the difficulties under which
you place me, by your sense of your own duty
and by your sacred pledge to his Royal Highness.
It happened that I was in the king's presence
when your letter, directed to be delivered immediately, was brought to me, and by his Majesty's
condescension I availed myself of the opportunity

of a comparison of opinion with him. The king was alarmed at the idea of the duke being depressed and disheartened by the most remote hint of his present danger, and was pleased to express his perfect approbation of my determination to use my own judgment as to the moment when I shall dare to disclose to his brother my conviction of the fatal issue of his malady.

" Pray forgive me if I differ from you in opinion upon this important point to the duke's safety, and be assured that I know of no human being who would go farther than yourself, my dear Taylor, to add an atom to the duke's comfort or to protract his valuable life an hour beyond the limits to which it is destined.

" I am, with the truest regard, my dear Taylor,
" Yours faithfully,

" HENRY HALFORD."

Sir HERBERT TAYLOR to Sir HENRY HALFORD.

" HORSE GUARDS, *August* 21*st*, 1826.

" MY DEAR SIR HENRY,

" I received your letter on Saturday morning, and I need not assure you, that feeling the full force of your reasoning, I went to Brighton with the determination to observe your injunctions.

" The enclosed copy of a letter which I had the honour of forwarding to his Majesty this morning will put you in full possession of all that has passed, and I sincerely hope that its contents will be satisfactory to you, and that you will give me the credit for having acted with due caution and discretion in the embarrassing and trying situation in which I was placed.

"I have no hesitation in saying to you that H.R.H.'s conversation was unreserved as to the possibility of a fatal result, but he is sanguine as to the strength of his constitution and other favourable counteracting symptoms, and I feel very forcibly that it would be cruel and mischievous to raise the alarm, while these favourable symptoms continue to hold out the least hope. But depend upon it, my dear Sir Henry, H.R.H. has firmness of mind sufficient to bear the disclosure whenever it shall appear to you necessary, and to meet the results. He appears indeed at present very sanguine, but he courts every opportunity of obtaining information. He does not shrink from the contemplation of his case in its most unfavourable light.

"H.R.H. told me, that if further change of air should be considered advisable, he would give a preference to Kew. He also said that Saturday would suit him just as well as Sunday to come to town. He spoke with gratitude of your kind and affectionate attention to him, and with satisfaction of the prospect of seeing you on Sunday and hearing from you whether he had gained or lost ground.

"Believe me to be ever, with the truest regards, my dear Sir Henry.

"Most faithfully yours,

"C. H. TAYLOR."

"WISTOW, *August 26th*, 1826.

" MY DEAR TAYLOR,

"I feel deeply obliged to you for your kindness on the subject of our late correspondence, and most particularly for letting me see your most candid, most interesting report to his Majesty, of the actual state in which you found and left the duke at Brighton subsequently to my visit.

"When I spoke so decidedly in deprecation of a communication to my patient of the danger of his disease, I would not that you understood it to be my meaning that the time would never arrive when H.R.H. should know that I expected a fatal issue of his symptoms. God forbid that either he or any human being should leave this world without being apprised that their last hour were approaching, and that they should prepare themselves for the change they were about to undergo. But I thought the struggle was making at this instant between the strength of the disease and the power of the constitution ; and I felt sure that this battle must be fought to a great disadvantage, if the mind were depressed. We have seen more than once in the course of this most interesting case, the sad consequences of moral influence upon the malady, and I felt as you do, that I had a duty to perform by availing myself of every advantage to be obtained by keeping up the duke's spirits and his hopes.

"Alas ! I fear that it will not be long ere your interposition is called for by myself, and that you will too soon have an opportunity of redeeming the sacred pledge you gave him ; for I assure you in the same spirit in which you made your promise to the duke, I make mine now to you, that when I lose all further hopes of administering the resources of our art to him with good effect, I will not only consent to your making the communication, but will invite you to make it.

"I am rejoiced to hear that the duke is not altogether averse to Kew, and I earnestly wish he might be prevailed upon to go there at once from Brighton, without stopping in Arlington Street, but this perhaps is hardly possible. I have written to H.R.H. to say that he may depend upon my keeping my appointment on Sunday, and I trust I shall soon find an opportunity of conversing with you and telling you my opinion of H.R.H.'s comparative state. Pray continue to believe me to be, with high esteem,

"My dear Taylor, yours faithfully,

"HENRY HALFORD."

The disease of the duke continued to make progress, the dropsical swelling to increase, and there were evident signs of water in the abdomen. After mature deliberation, it was resolved to endeavour to relieve the difficulty of breathing and to lessen the pressure from above upon the extremities. The operation of tapping was performed

on the 3rd of September, and about three gallons
of fluid were let out. His Royal Highness bore the
operation with the same resolution and quiet
composure which had marked his conduct under
every stage of his illness. For some days he
remained very weak, the left leg continuing in a
state that occasioned serious uneasiness. In about
a fortnight, however, H.R.H. gained strength, the
appetite and sleep returned, and on the 19th of
September he was enabled to resume his daily
airings in a carriage, which were continued till the
middle of October.

The hopes thus engendered proved, however,
delusive. The legs became worse, the constitu-
tional powers gave way, the appetite and sleep
began to fail, and during the whole month of
November the situation of the royal sufferer was
becoming daily more critical : and he was visibly
losing strength and substance. About the middle
of December the weakness increased and attacks of
faintness came on, announcing the nearer approach
of danger. On the 20th of December his Royal
Highness received the sacrament for the second
time, and during the whole of the solemn ceremony nothing could exceed his attention and calm
devotion. At this time the following letter was
addressed to the king by Sir Henry Halford :

"ARLINGTON STREET, *December 22nd*, 1826.

"SIRE,

"The total want of power to get down nourishment, and the languor which prevailed all yesterday in consequence, have produced a considerable effect for the worse in the Duke of York's case, and I am grieved to inform your Majesty that we consider H.R.H.'s situation is one of less hope than ever. It is true that there are no symptoms at present of immediate and instant danger to his invaluable life, but H.R.H. is in such a state as to make it probable that signs of pressing hazard may come on at any time.

"His Royal Highness appears to be so anxious to see things in a favourable light, and his frame is so directly influenced by the suspicion of an ill opinion of his circumstances, on the part of his medical attendants, that I dare not permit an expression to escape me which H.R.H. can construe into such a sense of his danger, as I have thought it my duty to convey in this letter to your Majesty; but I have at length permitted Sir H. Taylor to state to H.R.H. that he observes me to manifest a solicitude, a painful anxiety about him, which he has never observed in my countenance before.

"I am, Sire, most devotedly,

"Your Majesty's faithful servant,

"HENRY HALFORD."

The increased alarm and anxiety felt by his medical attendants was now imparted to H.R.H. by Sir Herbert Taylor, and he received the communication with pious resignation, exclaiming, " God's will be done; I am resigned."

From this time till the hour of his death, the difficulty of breathing and disposition to syncope, (during which neither the pulse nor the respiration were perceptible for a minute at a time,) became more urgent. During the night of January the 4th so serious an attack came on that it was thought all was over; but so great was the duke's tenacity of life and the power of his constitution, that he rallied, and in the morning took some nourishment. About twelve o'clock, though unable to speak, yet by looking at a clock which stood in the room and then at his legs, and by other signs intelligible, he gave his medical attendants to understand that he wished the daily dressing to be gone through. This wish, however useless now, was immediately complied with, and it evidently gave a satisfaction, which, alas ! could not be expressed. The pulse became more feeble, the attacks of faintness more frequent, and at twenty minutes past nine on the evening of January 5th the duke died.

I have given this case at such length, because

there are materials before me for doing so, which there are not of other members of the Royal Family; and especially as it conveys a clearer idea than could otherwise be given, of Sir Henry Halford's management and anxious care of those of his patients as were sick even unto death.

Sir Henry's attention to the Duke of York had been so unremitting, that to manifest the sense entertained of them in the highest quarter, he received by royal warrant a grant of armorial augmentations and supporters. His arms were previously: Argent, a greyhound passant sable, on a chief azure three fleurs-de-lis, or. For the central fleur-de-lis was substituted a rose argent; and in further augmentation was added on a canton ermine, a staff entwined with a serpent proper, and ensigned with a coronet composed of crosses patée and fleurs-de-lis (being that of a prince of the blood royal). As a crest of augmentation, a staff entwined with a serpent or, as on the canton. As supporters, two emews proper, each gorged with a coronet, composed of crosses patée and fleurs-de-lis. This is the only instance in English heraldry of the grant of supporters to a practising physician. As regards the particular supporters, it may be mentioned that

George IV. some time previously to this, had presented to Sir Henry Halford two fine emews that had been sent to him from abroad. These were forwarded to Wistow, where they proved to be very mischievous, and did much damage wherever they were. But this was borne with in consideration of their royal donor, and they were permitted to die a natural death. One of them, a very fine bird, stuffed and mounted, is still to be seen in a glazed case in the inner hall at Wistow. When the question of supporters was under consideration, Sir Henry's loyalty led him to suggest the emews, and they were at once assigned to him.

Sir Henry Halford, who had been occasionally consulted by the Prince of Wales in the course of 1810, was appointed in September of that year physician-in-ordinary to his Royal Highness.

"CARLTON HOUSE, *September 22nd*, 1810.

"SIR,

"I am commanded by the Prince of Wales to assure you that his Royal Highness feels a very high gratification in receiving you into the situation of one of his physicians-in-ordinary. The public consideration in which you are held, as well as the personal esteem

his Royal Highness entertains for you, could not
fail to secure the object of your wishes.

" I have the honour to be, Sir,

" Your most obedient and most humble servant,

"B. BLOOMFIELD."

" To Sir HENRY HALFORD, Bart."

From that time Sir Henry was in regular,
almost daily, attendance on his Royal Highness,
whose confidence in Sir Henry's medical skill
was unbounded, and to whom he then and
thenceforward entrusted the care and management of his health. Sir Henry's prominent
position in the profession and with the Prince
Regent, made him the subject of amusing comment by the wits of the time. Among such, the
following lines, said to be by Henry Luttrell, may
be selected :

"The Regent, sir, is taken ill,
  And all depends on Halford's skill.
 'Pray what,' inquired that sage physician,
 'Has brought him to this sad condition?'
 When Bloomfield ventured to pronounce
 A little too much Cherry Bounce.

 The Regent, hearing what was said,
 Raised from the couch his aching head,
 And cried, 'No, Halford, 'tis not so—
 Cure us, O Doctor—Curaçoa.'"

Sir Walter Farquhar, Sir Gilbert Blane, Sir
William Knighton, Sir Matthew Tierney and

Dr. H. H. Southey, all of whom were in succession on the medical staff of the Prince Regent and of George IV. as physicians-in-ordinary to the person, were occasionally but rarely called into consultation with Sir Henry Halford. The ordinary regular care of the the king's health as well before as after his accession to the throne, was confided to Sir Henry Halford. With him Sir Matthew Tierney was for the most part associated, whenever from .any cause, additional aid was needed. He was acceptable to the king and was in entire accord with Sir Henry Halford in his view of the medical treatment needed by their royal master.

Sir Matthew Tierney was born in the sister island, and came of an old and respectable family in the county of Limerick. In 1798 he was appointed by the Earl of Berkeley, to whom he had been recently introduced, surgeon to his lordship's regiment of militia. In 1802 he settled as a physician at Brighton, and was presented by his patron Lord Berkeley to the Prince of Wales, who some time subsequently appointed him physician to his Royal Highness's household there.

The Prince was subject at that time to fulness of blood, and to several of the severer symptoms consequent thereon. On those occasions he had derived such immediate and signal relief from loss of blood, that he was prone to fly to it on slight attacks even without medical sanction, and, as Sir Henry Halford thought, unwisely and too frequently. Under such circumstances, Sir Henry left distinct directions at Brighton, that the prince was not to be bled under any circumstances but in his presence or with his sanction. On one occasion, the Prince after a restless night, was attacked early in the morning with great anguish and load about the chest in addition to other symptoms with which he was more familiar. As Sir Henry could not then be procured from London in less than twelve hours at the least, and the symptoms were more than ordinarily urgent, the Prince was importunate for that relief, which he felt nothing but bleeding could give him, and accordingly sent for Sir Matthew (then Dr.) Tierney, who seeing that prompt relief was urgently needed, directed venesection and took away a large amount of blood with immediate and marked relief to all the Prince's sufferings. Sir Henry, on his arrival at Brighton some hours after, was disposed at first to blame and resent this infraction of his directions ; but, as the result of his consultation with Dr. Tierney, admitted frankly that the practice under the circumstances was correct and had been in every respect successful. Dr. Tierney thus secured the favour of the Prince and the confidence of Sir Henry Halford. In 1816 he was appointed physician-in-ordinary to the Prince Regent and was created a baronet, 3rd October, 1818. In the medical arrangements consequent on the accession of George IV. he was gazetted one of the physicians-in-ordinary to the king ; and was continued in the like high office by William IV., who created him a knight commander of the royal Guelphic order of Hanover. Sir Matthew Tierney was in attendance with Sir Henry Halford during the last illness and at the death of both of his royal masters.

The health of the Prince Regent had not, for some time, been satisfactory, and in a day or two after his accession to the throne—on the 29th January, 1820—his Majesty was struck down with an acute illness. The king had been ailing for some days with a severe cold, and on January 31st his symptoms assumed an alarming aspect. He had been attacked with inflammation of the lungs and was attended by Sir Henry Halford, Sir William Knighton, and Sir Matthew Tierney. Under active medical treatment at the onset of the inflammation, the disease was brought under control, and thenceonwards ran a normal course, so that by 10th February the King "was free from complaint" and no more bulletins were issued.

The funeral of George III. had been fixed for the 15th of February, 1820, and the king, George IV., although but just recovering from a severe attack of inflammation of the lungs, decided himself to be present on that occasion. The peril in doing so was so great that two of his Majesty's physicians, Sir Henry Halford and Sir William Knighton, interposed in the following letter of protest and supplication, and with the desired effect of inducing the king to desist from his intention :

"SIRE—

"We, your Majesty's physicians, venture humbly to approach your Majesty to implore your Majesty to forego that satisfaction to your feelings which your Majesty attaches to a performance of the last act of filial piety to the late king, your Majesty's father.

"We are scarcely yet relieved from that state of anxiety and alarm which your Majesty's dangerous illness gave rise to, and from which your Majesty is only just extricated under the mercy of heaven.

"We cannot therefore contemplate an indulgence of your Majesty's wishes without absolute dismay, seeing the probability of a relapse in consequence of the exposure of your Majesty's person to the night air in a cathedral, under that anguish of mind which your Majesty was observed by everybody so painfully to suffer, at the performance of the same sad ceremony last year.

"And we humbly entreat your Majesty to yield, not to our wishes only, but to those of the whole nation, which would be expressed, we are persuaded, if it were generally known that your Majesty meditated this dangerous effort of respect and piety.

"HENRY HALFORD,
WILLIAM KNIGHTON.

"CARLTON PALACE, *February 7th*, 1820."

During the whole ten years of the king's reign his Majesty's health was a subject of anxiety to his physicians, and especially to Sir Henry Halford, to whom exclusively in all ordinary circumstances the king was pleased to entrust the medical charge of himself. It was generally known that his Majesty's health had been in an unsatisfactory state for a considerable period, but as it did not render confinement necessary, it did not excite alarm until directions were given in consequence of the increase of the malady, to countermand the preparations for the festivities with whicth he royal birthday was to have been celebrated at Court in April. It had been known for some time by the physicians that the king had disease of the heart, which could have no other than a fatal termination, and its course, which was very similar to that of the Duke of York, was foreseen and anticipated.

The first bulletin was issued on the 15th of April, and announced that his Majesty was suffering under a bilious attack, accompanied by embarrassment of breathing. The symptoms varied a good deal from time to time, his Majesty enjoying temporary intervals of comparative ease, but they were not giving way, and brought with them such bodily debility as rendered even the slightest personal exertion painful. Additional symptoms which manifested a breaking-up of the constitution, and foremost among these, dropsy, began to show themselves, and after a time puncturing of the legs was had recourse to, and gave temporary relief. The king suffered, too, from violent attacks of coughing, so severe that on more occasions than one, death appeared to be imminent. The king died early in the morning of Saturday, June 26th, 1830, and more suddenly than was expected. Feeling a sudden thrill of pain he exclaimed, " This is death ! send directly for Halford"; and the king expired in the act of making a friendly inclination of the head to Sir Henry on his entering the apartment.*

The physicians who had been in attendance on the king were sharply criticised in some of the public prints for the bulletins they had issued, which it was argued were calculated, even if they were not intended, to mislead. Sir Henry Halford availed himself of an early opportunity to refute the imputation, and justify himself and his colleagues for their part on that occasion; and at the same time he considered generally the conduct and duty of the physician towards a patient suffering from mortal disease. In an elegant essay " On the Influence of some Diseases of the Body on the Mind," which he read at one of the evening meetings of the College of Physicians in February, 1831, he said: "You will forgive me perhaps if I presume to state what appears to me to be the conduct proper to be observed by a physician, in withholding or making his patient acquainted with his opinion of the probable issue of a malady manifesting mortal symptoms. I own, I think it my first duty to protract his life by all practicable means, and to

* Lord Stanhope's " Notes of Conversations with the Duke of Wellington." 8vo. London, 1888, p. 257.

interpose myself between him and everything which may possibly aggravate his danger.*   And unless I shall have found him averse from doing what was necessary in aid of my remedies, from a want of a proper sense of his perilous situation, I forbear to step out of the bounds of my province in order to offer any advice which is not necessary to promote his cure.   At the same time, I think it indispensable to let his friends know the danger of his case the instant I discover it.   An arrangement of his worldly affairs, in which the comfort or unhappiness of those who are to come after him is involved, may be necessary; and a suggestion of his danger, by which the accomplishment of this object is to be obtained, naturally induces a contemplation of his more important spiritual concerns, a more careful review of his past life, and such sincere sorrow and contrition for what he has done amiss, as justifies our humble hope of his pardon and acceptance hereafter.   If friends can do their good offices at a proper time, and under the suggestions of the

* "At hoc ne homines probi faciunt, ut amicis impendentes calamitates prædicant, quas illi effugere nullo modo possint : et medici, quamquam intelligunt sæpe, tamen nunquam ægris dicunt illo morbo eos esse morituros. Omnis enim prædictio mali tumprobatur cum ad prædictionem cautio adjungitur."— CICERO, "De Divinatione," ii. 25.

physician, it is far better that they should undertake them than the medical adviser. They do so
without destroying his hopes, for the patient will
still believe that he has an appeal to his physician
beyond their fears ; whereas, if the physician lay
open his danger to him, however delicately he
may do this, he runs a risk of appearing to pronounce a sentence of condemnation to death,
against which there is no appeal, *no hope ;* and *on
that account*, what is most awful to think of,
perhaps the sick man's repentance may be less
available.

"But friends may be absent, and nobody near
the patient in his extremity, of sufficient influence
or pretension to inform him of his dangerous
condition. And surely it is lamentable to think
that any human being should leave the world
unprepared to meet his Creator and Judge, 'with
all his crimes broad blown.' Rather than so, I
have departed from my strict professional duty,
and have done that which I would have done by
myself, and have apprised my patient of the great
change he was about to undergo.

"In short, no rule, not to be infringed sometimes, can be laid down on this subject. Every
case requires its own considerations ; but you may
be assured, that if good sense and good feeling be

not wanting, no difficulty can occur which you will not be able to surmount with satisfaction to your patient, his friends and yourselves.

"Advice on some of these points, at least, corresponding with that which I have presumed to offer you, is to be found in the beautiful chapter of Hippocrates, περι ευσχημοσυνής—de decenti ornatu; and I assure you it will amply repay you for the trouble of referring to it, by the gravity and striking propriety of deportment which it recommends.

" But if, in cases attended with danger in private life, the physician has need of discretion and sound sense to direct his conduct, the difficulty must doubtless be increased when his patient is of so *elevated a station that his safety becomes an object of anxiety to the nation.* In such circumstances, the physician has a duty to perform, not only to the sick personage and his family, but also to the public, who, in their extreme solicitude for his recovery, sometimes desire disclosures which are incompatible with it. Bulletins respecting the health of a sovereign, differ widely from the announcements which a physician is called upon to make in humbler life, and which he entrusts to the prudence of surrounding friends. These public documents may become known to the royal sufferer himself. Is the physician, then, whilst endeavouring to relieve the anxiety or satisfy the curiosity of the nation, to endanger the safety of the patient; or, at least, his comfort? Surely not. But whilst it is his object to state as accurately as possible the present circumstances and the comparative condition of the disease, he will consider that conjectures respecting its cause and probable issue are not to be hazarded without extreme caution. He will not write one word, which is calculated to mislead; but neither ought he to be called upon to express so much as, if reported to the patient, would destroy all hope and hasten that catastrophe which it is his duty and their first wish to prevent.

" Meanwhile, the family of the monarch and the government have a claim to fuller information than can, with propriety or even common humanity, be imparted to the public at large. In the case of his Majesty, King George the Fourth, the king's government and the Royal Family were apprised, as early as the 27th of April * (I hold in my hand the original letters which gave the information to the prime minister) that his Majesty's disease was seated in his heart, and that an effusion of water into the chest was soon

* His Majesty died on the 25th of June.

to be expected. It was not, however, until the latter end of May—when his Majesty was so discouraged by repeated attacks of embarrasment in his breathing, as to desire me to explain to him the nature of his complaint, and to give him my candid opinion of its probable termination—that the opportunity occurred of acknowledging to his Majesty the extent of my fears for his safety.

" This communication was not necessary to suggest to the king the propriety of religious offices, for his Majesty had used them daily. But it determined him, perhaps, to appoint an early day to receive the sacrament. He did receive it, with every appearance of the most fervent piety and devotion, and acknowledged to me repeatedly afterwards that it had given him great consolation—true comfort.

" After this, when ' he had set his house in order,' I thought myself at liberty to interpret every new symptom as it arose in as favourable a light as I could, for his Majesty's satisfaction ; and we were enabled thereby to rally his spirits in the intervals of his frightful attacks, to maintain his confidence in his medical resources, and to spare him the pain of contemplating approaching death, until a few minutes before his Majesty expired.

" Lord Bacon, one of the wisest men who has

lived, encourages physicians to make it a part of their art to smooth the bed of death, and to render the departure from life easy, placid, and gentle.

"This doctrine, so accordant with the best principles of our nature, commended not only by the wisdom of this consummate philosopher, but also by the experience of one of the most judicious and conscientious physicians of modern times, the late Dr. Heberden, was practised with such happy success in the case of our lamented sovereign that at the close of his painful disease, 'non tam mori videretur' (as was said of a Roman emperor) 'quam dulci et alto sopore excipi.'"

Among the visitors to the College of Physicians on that evening, and they were numerous, were the Lord Chancellor, the Archbishop of Canterbury, the Bishop of London, Lord Tenterden, the Vice-Chancellor, the Master of the Rolls, several others of the judges, the Attorney-General, and others. The general but subdued applause which followed the reading of Sir Henry Halford's explanation, showed that his audience appreciated his good feeling and correct taste, and accepted the rules of conduct he had laid down as the solution of one of the most delicate questions in medical ethics, and as those which ought always to guide the physician in his intercourse with his patient at the most momentous and trying period of his being—that last scene of human life in which every one, sooner or later, must appear and bear his part.

Soon after the decease of George IV., Sir Henry received another flattering proof of the esteem and appreciation of the Royal Family. A very splendid clock, surmounted by a bust of his late Majesty, was presented to him by the Royal Family, in evidence, as the inscription states, "of their esteem and regard, and in testimony of the high sense they entertain of his professional abilities and unwearied attention to their late beloved sister, the Princess Amelia, her late Majesty Queen Charlotte, his late Majesty King George III., his late Royal Highness the Duke of York, and lastly, to his Majesty George IV."

The kindly feeling of George IV. for Sir Henry Halford continued to the last. At the last interview which the Duke of Clarence had with George IV. the king requested of the duke as a personal favour to himself, that on his accession to the throne he would continue Sir Henry Halford in his office of first physician to the king, and the actual attendant upon himself. This was readily assented to, for the relations of the Duke of Clarence with Sir Henry, from the time when he first consulted him in the summer of 1811, had been at all times of the most satisfactory character.   Accordingly, in the medical appointments on the accession of William IV., Sir Henry Halford was gazetted first physician to the king, and first physician also to the queen.   And one of the first acts of William IV. was to confer on Sir Henry the Grand Cross of Hanover.   The Duke of Cambridge thereupon hastened to present him with the fitting decoration.

" BRIGHTON, September 5th, 1830.

" MY DEAR SIR HENRY,

"I hasten to send you the Star which I have this moment received from Mr. Bridge, and request you will accept it, as a mark of the sincere regard I have for you, and which can never end but with the life of him, whom you will ever find

" Yours most sincerely,

" ADOLPHUS FREDERICK."

The king enjoyed unusually good health, and only on rare occasions needed the aid of his physicians.   A slight decline in the king's strength had been perceptible to his immediate attendants at the commencement of 1837, but it was not until the month of May that the state of his Majesty's health excited any serious apprehension. On the 17th of May the king held a *levée*, and on the 18th a drawing-room, at St. James's Palace, and on his return to Windsor Castle on both of these occasions showed signs of great debility and exhaustion, with oppression of breathing and considerable difficulty in ascending stairs. The king was then attended by his domestic physician, Dr. David Davies. To the above symptoms were soon added entire loss of appetite and attacks of faintness. This state of his Majesty excited much and well-founded alarm.

On Monday, May 22nd, Sir Henry Halford was summoned to the king at Windsor, and Dr. Chambers was sent for at the same time, but unknown to the king, and unknown also to Sir Henry, who arrived at the castle in the course of the afternoon and was at once ushered to the king.

The feelings of Queen Adelaide towards Sir Henry Halford were known to be of a less cordial and confidential nature than he had been honoured with by the king himself and all the other members of the Royal Family, and he was pained at the scant confidence accorded to him on this occasion.

In the "Annual Register" for 1837 are "Some Recollections of the last Days of his late Majesty King William IV.," dated Bushey House, July 14, 1837, and evidently inspired, if not dictated, by one of the highest personages in the realm; wherein we read : " Sir Henry Halford and Dr. Chambers were sent for, but as the latter had no ostensible situation in the royal household, it was thought advisable, in order to avoid causing any unnecessary alarm to the king, to introduce him to his Majesty as the medical attendant on the queen.   Dr. Chambers was most graciously received by the king, who did not hesitate to avail himself of his advice in his own case.   The arrival, however, of Dr. Chambers at the castle was so late that this interview did not take place till the following morning," when Sir Henry Halford and Dr. Chambers saw the king together, and from that time were one or other of them in constant attendance on his Majesty ; Sir Henry during the day, Dr. Chambers through the night, each of them remaining until relieved by the arrival of the other at the castle.   At a later period Sir Matthew Tierney was joined with them in attendance on the king.   It was not until June 9th that the king consented that a bulletin should be issued by his physicians to allay, if possible, the anxiety which had long been felt and manifested by the public. It was as follows :

"WINDSOR CASTLE, *June 9th*, 1837.

"The king has suffered for some time from an affection of the chest, which confines his Majesty to his apartment, and has produced considerable weakness, but has not interrupted his usual attention to business.

"(Signed)

"HENRY HALFORD,
WM. FRED. CHAMBERS."

The weakness went on increasing—augmented difficulty of breathing, progressive failure of the circulation, cold extremities, and swelling of the legs, were among the symptoms which evinced that the king's condition had now become one of extreme danger. The king's government was desirous that the public should be duly prepared for any event that might happen, and the prime minister addressed the following letter to Sir Henry Halford :

"SOUTH STREET, *June 12th*, 1837.

"MY DEAR SIR HENRY,

"The accounts which I have received from Windsor in the course of the day are by no means favourable. Sir H. Taylor writes to me to this effect, and others who have come up from thence confirm his report.   In these circumstances I am very anxious that no chance should be run of any event occurring, for which the public is not prepared.

"If the king should be better to-morrow, or if he shall remain, in point of health, exactly stationary, which is hardly probable, another bulletin may be delayed until Wednesday ; but if he should be the least worse, I think that some information should be given to the public.   I have written to Dr. Chambers this evening to this effect.

"I understand that the bulletin of this morning is generally interpreted by the public as being very unfavourable, which is much better than the contrary.   More than one person in the House of Lords said to me, 'Of course he had a very bad night, as the bulletin says nothing upon the subject.'

"Yours faithfully,

"MELBOURNE.

"Sir HENRY HALFORD, Bart."

But for a day or two there was if anything an amelioration in the king's condition.   On the 16th, however, he was more feeble, and on the 17th he was worse in every respect.   The weakness went on increasing, and on June 19th the following bulletin was issued :

"The King continues in a very weak and feeble

state, notwithstanding his Majesty had some quiet sleep in the night. After transacting his usual business yesterday, his Majesty received the sacrament from the hands of the Archbishop of Canterbury with attention and great apparent comfort.

"HENRY HALFORD,
MATT. JOHN TIERNEY,
WM. FRED. CHAMBERS,
DAVID DAVIES."

In the course of the following night the king died.

"WINDSOR CASTLE, *Tuesday, June 20th*, 1837.

"It has pleased Almighty God to release from his sufferings our gracious sovereign King William the Fourth. His Majesty expired this morning at twelve minutes past two o'clock.

"MATT. JOHN TIERNEY,
WM. FRED. CHAMBERS,
DAVID DAVIES."

Sir Henry Halford, under the arrangement above mentioned, was not on duty when the king actually expired, and did not therefore sign the above bulletin. He received from Dr. Chambers the following letter:

"WINDSOR CASTLE, *Tuesday morning*, 3 A.M.

"MY DEAR SIR HENRY,

"The scene has at length closed. The poor

king expired at twelve minutes past two o'clock
this morning in the most tranquil manner possible.
The absolute process of dissolution did not commence till about eleven o'clock, but from that
hour his Majesty sank rapidly.   No new symptom
occurred before death.

"The archbishop, who remained here, accompanied (at the queen's desire) Lord Conyngham (?)
to announce Her accession to the young Princess.

"The Queen has borne this scene with great
self-possession, and is now gone to bed in a
composed state of mind.

"I find I am too late for Lord Melbourne's
messenger, who has already set off, so that this
note will not be the means of conveying to you
the first account of his Majesty's death : as,
however, I have written thus far, I send my note
to you.   Believe me, my dear Sir Henry,

"Yours faithfully,

"W. F. CHAMBERS.

"Sir HENRY HALFORD, Bart., Curzon Street."

Sir Henry would seem to have hesitated for a
moment about returning that day to Windsor to
offer his respects to the Queen Adelaide, or at the
least personally to inquire for her Majesty's health.
If he really did so, all doubts must have been dis-
pelled by the following note from his sincere and
constant friend, the Duke of Cumberland, or, as
he had then become, the King of Hanover :

"GLOUCESTER HOUSE, 10 A.M., *June 20th*, 1837.

"DEAR SIR HENRY,

"I hope you will excuse an old and sincere friend observing to you the propriety of your going down to Windsor, if only *to inquire after the queen;* and at the same time I take it for granted the body will be opened, when surely you as HIS *first and confidential* medical adviser ought to be present.   Excuse this, but attribute it to true friendship.

"Yours very sincerely,

"ERNEST."

Sir Henry had continued to attend the king with his Majesty's undiminished confidence until he died.   Queen Adelaide recognised his services on this occasion in the inscription engraved on a large silver vase elaborately wrought which, as Queen Dowager, she presented to Sir Henry shortly after the king's death :

TO

SIR HENRY HALFORD, BART. G.C.H.

A GRATEFUL ACKNOWLEDGMENT

OF HIS ATTENDANCE UPON

HIS LATE MAJESTY

KING WILLIAM IV.

DURING HIS LAST ILLNESS.

A. R.

Sir Henry Halford was emphatically "the

friend of the Royal Family," as he was declared to be by the Prince Regent himself to Miss Knight, when that lady wished to prevent or abridge the long conferences which Sir Henry, with the approval of the Prince Regent, was at one time having with the Princess Charlotte of Wales.

Sir Henry's intimate relations with the several members of the Royal Family and their entire confidence in him, led to his being called on not unfrequently to undertake offices which had no connection with his profession.

He was actively engaged in 1815 in the attempt to bring about a reconciliation between Queen Charlotte and the Duke of Cumberland, who had displeased her Majesty by his marriage. Sir Henry, too, was the medium of communication between the Prince Regent and the Princess Charlotte in all that related to the project of her marriage with the Prince of Orange. Sir Henry had been in medical attendance on the princess during the early part of 1813, and in October of that year hints were given to the princess by Sir Henry, at the request of the Prince Regent, that such a marriage would be highly desirable; but as is well known this project in the end came to nothing, and was terminated by the princess herself in June 1814.

Sir Henry Halford's active connection with the court ceased with the death of William IV. He was continued one of the physicians-in-ordinary to the Queen ; but the office of first physician and of actual attendant on the sovereign, passed not unnaturally nor unexpectedly, into other and younger hands, into those of Dr. (subsequently Sir James) Clark, who from the death of Dr. Maton had been the trusted and valued physician to the Princess Victoria and to H.R.H. the Duchess of Kent.

Sir Henry Halford had been physician to and the actual medical attendant on George III., George IV. and William IV.—on the Queen Charlotte—on all the royal dukes and on all the princesses ; and it had been his melancholy privilege to minister at the death-bed of no less than seven of the Royal Family. He is said also to have been consulted at various times, and particularly in 1814, by several of the potentates of Europe. I know of no other physician of ancient or modern times of whom there is such a record.

CHAPTER VIII

SIR HENRY HALFORD from an early period of his professional life was much given to letter-writing. He continued to be so even when in his fullest business, and indeed until strength began to fail him. He maintained a frequent correspondence with many members of the Royal Family, and with many of the noblest and most distinguished of the land, most of whom had been his patients, and in sequel thereto had become his friends and correspondents. It was so I believe in all the following instances. Many of his letters were written in his carriage in the course of his professional rounds about town, or in his longer journeys into the country : but most of them after the other duties of the day, and often after midnight. Of his own letters, there are but few comparatively before me, but those from his correspondents are many and interesting. Among such are the following. They will I believe bear me out in the opinion I have formed and expressed, of the character and attainments, the position and influence, professional and social, of Sir Henry Halford.

The Duke of Cumberland had early honoured Sir Henry Halford with his esteem and friendship. From among a large number of his letters I select the following. The first two of them relate to the efforts Sir Henry was making in 1815, to effect a reconciliation between the queen and the duke, who had displeased her Majesty by his marriage.

The Duke of Cumberland to Sir Henry Halford.

"*Thursday night*, 12 *o'clock* P.M.

"Dear Halford,

"Your letter was safely received this evening at half-past eight, and you may rest assured will be kept most secret. I am desired to return you many thanks for it and to say, *you* will be expected with anxiety here on Sunday by eleven o'clock, and as you come to town Saturday, pray direct a line here : the uprightness and straightforwardness of your conduct must demand the respect of every one, and of none more than of

"Yours very sincerely,

"Ernest."

"KEW GREEN, *October 27th,* 1815.

"DEAR HALFORD,

"Your very kind letter I received yesterday, and communicated its contents, with all its kind wishes to the duchess, who equally with myself, feels grateful to you, for all your endeavours, and I trust and hope most sincerely—nay, from something that I heard yesterday—I still flatter myself that better days will come ; for as far as I can make out, her heart feels deeply the mischief she has done—the cruelty with which she has treated us ; this seems perfectly correct from what you have stated. I therefore do from my very soul believe that by often and often repeating the misery she so generally has occasioned and still causes to us, that her heart will at length feel the injustice, and she will seize an opportunity of trying to make everything smooth and right again ; and in order that she may find less difficulty, from an idea of anything unpleasant being said, both the duchess and myself are desirous to save her feelings on that point, that whenever the happy day of reconciliation shall take place, that not one word on this unpleasant subject shall be uttered by either party. Now I flatter myself this is a just proof that we desire to make the matter as easy to the queen as possible.

"With respect to what you say, of perhaps its having been better had *I* gone in the first instance myself to the queen, I will not be obstinate and say *I was right*, but really and truly my indignation was so roused by this unexpected letter, that I did not in the first instance trust myself, that my temper being rather warm might not have got the better of my judgment, and I might have made things worse. And secondly, I did not think that going to her after her explicit declaration would have been treating my wife with the respect due to her. And to prove that I am justified in this idea, the queen herself said to the P., 'he could not do otherwise.'

"Excuse my having troubled you again, but your so friendly and kind letter demanded from me an answer, and most indisputably my warmest thanks. In case you cannot call next Wednesday, I depend on seeing you next Friday.

"Believe me, dear Halford,

"Yours very sincerely,

"ERNEST."

From the time the duke became King of Hanover and left England he maintained a frequent correspondence of an easy and confidential character with Sir Henry Halford. Of these letters the following are perhaps the most generally interesting :

The King of Hanover to Sir Henry Halford.

"Hanover, *September 9th,* 1839.

"Dear Sir Henry,

"... . As to myself, I am wonderfully well considering the total change of life I am forced to live, and the constant worry I have now lived in ever since I first took the reins of government. Heaven has so far till now aided my honest endeavours, and by never swerving from my principles but acting always under the law, I have just succeeded in carrying the first victory ; having given the German Radicals the first check they have had since the year 1830. Strange things are going on, alas ! in dear old England, and my heart bleeds on hearing all going on and the levelling system that seems the order of the day.

"Yours very truly

"Ernest."

The following has reference to the sight of the Prince Royal. Baron de Graefe had been summoned to Hanover to consult on the case of the prince, and perform such operation as might seem advisable. But he was attacked on the evening of his arrival with the usual symptoms of typhus fever, which proved fatal within a fortnight.

"HANOVER, *July* 14*th*, 1840.

" DEAR SIR HENRY,

"Accept my best thanks for yours received this day, and the contents of your letter are certainly more cheering. God grant of his infinite mercy that you may be able to continue to give me so much more tranquillising accounts of the amendment.

" After the truly lamentable death of Dr. de Graefe, which has been a dreadful blow to us all, I had among my other difficulties to consider what was best to be done, and I therefore called upon the faculty here to consider maturely what proposals they would make as to the performance of the operation upon the Prince Royal. They have recommended to me an oculist of great repute at Vienna, a Dr. Jaeger, and I have directed them to write to him, communicate the state of the eye and complaint, and ask him if he will come and perform the operation, and I now expect in a short time his reply.

" The medical men have acted most honourably : they said, ' Here at Hanover Dr. Spangenberg is fully competent to undertake it ; he has now attended the Prince Royal for three years, is perfectly master of the case and is an excellent operator, but he is not a renowned man in the medical world as the late Dr. Graefe was, and as Dr. Jaeger is, therefore it is our public duty to recommend one whose reputation is universally known, and we therefore submit his name to you.

" I believe I have done the most prudent thing, and naturally, previous to deciding, I consulted my son's feelings, *who* is the most concerned.

" Believe me, dear Sir Henry,

" Yours very truly,

" ERNEST."

In the following month, August 8th, 1840, he writes as follows :

" Strange, and I may say as the author says, 'most wondrous strange,' that so many things occurred on the *first* of August ; for on that self-same day that our family came to the throne of Great Britain, *I* signed and sealed the *soi-disant* new constitution, or revised the old one amended, and thus after a state of constant anxiety for three full years have carried my point and, though I say it myself, I have been the *first* and *only* man here in Germany who stood up and opposed the Radicals of Germany. I received this day a most beautiful letter from the King of Prussia congratulating me. . . .

" I am going now for one week to a shooting-box I have about 100 miles from hence, merely to prevent eternal audiences and conferences ; when I mean to go about in my woods and try to shoot some roebucks and not occupy myself with state affairs or politics, for I have had enough of them to satiate me. Oh ! how often do I sigh after dear Kew and my little cottage there.

There is a great deal of glory but little enjoy-
ment in a king's life, and as Duke of Cumberland
I was much happier and more my own master,
than I now shall ever be again, but my heart and
my principles remain the same, and also my
sincere regard for you.

"Yours very truly,

"ERNEST."

In another of August 22nd, 1840, he writes :

"You are very good to think of my troubles
here, which under the blessing of Providence I
believe now I have overcome, but believe me it
has been a dead weight on my mind and given
me many a restless hour ; for till now I have
been left to shift for myself and had to encounter
every difficulty that man could have, but my
salvo has been that the country in itself is good
and not corrupted as yet, which are my great
support and give me the courage to go on and
carry me through my labour.   My good luck has
been, and what I have constantly acknowledged
is, to have served a thirty years' apprenticeship
in an English parliament, and the constant attendance to my parliamentary duties has given me a
complete insight and knowledge of what the
wants really are, and thus I am able to combat
these—Radicals.

"My friends in England all are violent against
me, but I knew what I was about and would not

allow myself to be diverted from the line I had begun; and though assailed from my old friends in England and many others not to continue, I never did, and was fully persuaded that I must succeed in the end; doubtfulness or weakness shown on my side would have been destruction, and I boldly went on, but was ever prudent and cautious, and thus always had my feet well secured ere I proceeded further. *Now* I am assailed with congratulations from every quarter, and they go so far as to tell me I have been the only king who could have stemmed the democratic spirit here on the continent; my reply is very short—is this so? then aid me and stand by me. The fact is they are not made for, or understand representative governments, and this has cost much blood in England to learn it, which God forbid may ever be the case here on the continent."

The Queen of Hanover died the 21st of June, 1841. The following is the king's letter to Sir Henry Halford in reference to that event:

" HANOVER, July 25th, 1841.

" DEAR SIR HENRY,

" Your kind letter of the 15th I should not have postponed answering so long, unless I had been absolutely prevented by the wretched state of spirits I am in, by the constant stretch of bodily and moral exertion I am forced to make in order to get through a mass of business, and then be able to think of my health, for certainly the anguish of soul and anxiety of mind I have gone through, the living between fear and hope, all has made a deep ravage in me, and I begin to feel I am giving way ; for when I reflect coolly on all I have now these last four years been obliged to go through, the eternal strain of mind—the constant difficulties thrown in my way—I hardly can believe that I have been able to effect all I have done ; but what then supported me was a happy home, domestic felicity—this is gone, and gone for ever, never to be recovered.   The agitation in which I lived upwards of three months has ruined my constitution, strong and hale as heaven had endowed me with, and I now feel I am giving way— an affection of the trachea—for I do not know how otherwise to explain it, comes on at times, a sort of cramp in the lower part of my throat, which causes me violent fits of coughing.   I have no pain in my chest, nor other expectoration than phlegm ; this they tell me the waters of Emms will remedy.   I have therefore resolved, though reluctantly to try them, for I would much rather remain quietly here.   As you knew my adored, beloved wife, you know *all* I have *lost*.   God be merciful to me.

" Yours faithfully,

" ERNEST."

The following letters, in addition to one already given (p. 136), are from the Duke of Kent:

"WINDSOR CASTLE,
Monday morning, December 20*th.*

"MY DEAR SIR HENRY,

"I cannot leave this without writing a few lines to express my warmest acknowledgments for your most interesting detail of the state of my poor suffering Sophy, and assuring you that I appreciate your kindness in writing to me, more than I can express. Understanding that you are to be here to-night and will return in the morning, forgive me if I entreat you to write me a line to-morrow per post from town to Kensington to say how you leave her, as it is a most anxious time, and the receiving your own account will be so much superior to anything else.

"May I also beg leave to remind you of a commission Minny gave you concerning a souvenir I would wish to give my old friend Dundas, as I am most solicitous not to postpone it longer than is unavoidable.

"With many apologies for all the trouble I am giving you, and every sentiment of the most friendly regard and the highest esteem,

"I remain, my dear Sir Henry,

"Yours most faithfully and sincerely,

"EDWARD."

"THE LODGE, CASTLE HILL,
Friday, January 28*th,* 1814.

"I owe you a thousand thanks, my dear Sir Henry, for your kind recollection of me, which I received yesterday evening. I cannot deny that the account it contained of my poor little suffering favourite rather disappointed me, as from her being apparently better on Sunday and Monday I had been rather too sanguine in flattering myself that we had begun to gain ground, which fond expectation, alas! I perceive is not realised. However, it is always consoling to read your opinions, so perfectly and candidly expressed as they ever are; and I feel most grateful for them, as well as for your increasing tender care of your poor patient.

"I perfectly understand all you say about the difficulty of making a certain quarter understand the real state of things, but when there is a natural want of warmth, it is difficult in the extreme to make a proper impression. Thank God! all are not alike on this head.

"Sincerely hoping you have escaped the late dreadful travelling,* both on the road and through the streets, without accident, and that your mind is now quite at ease about your son, I beg leave to subscribe myself, with every sentiment of the warmest friendship, regard and esteem,

"My dear Sir,

"Yours faithfully,

"EDWARD."

* The deep snow and frost of 1814.

"The Lodge, Castle Hill,
February 12th, 1814.

" My dear Sir Henry,

"I am anxious to express to you all the gratitude I feel for your most feeling and interesting account of our dear sufferer, and which was doubly gratifying, as the preceding one from dearest Minny had been far from consoling. Thank God, your visit was productive of so much good, and I now anxiously pray for the continuance of this improvement.

"To-morrow I shall ride over, and you will easily believe shall feel most grateful if I don't find her altered for the worse, in the three weeks I have not seen her. . . .

"I heard with great concern of the prince's severe attack. I hope he knows I called on him Saturday week, and again on Thursday. About Tuesday I shall hope to have the pleasure of seeing him. In the meanwhile will you have the goodness to say all that is respectful and affectionate from me (though I fear from a hint I have had, that an attempt has again been made to misrepresent me to him), but this is quite *entre nous*.

"Sincerely hoping that your son ere this is completely re-established in his health, I shall now take my leave of you by repeating the sentiments of grateful and friendly regard with which I am,

" My dear Sir Henry,

" Most affectionately yours,

" Edward."

The following letters are from the Duke of Cambridge ; who, at the time they were written, was Viceroy of Hanover :

"HANOVER, *December 27th*, 1813.

" I cannot suffer this opportunity to pass, without troubling you with a few lines, my dear Sir Henry, to thank you for your very kind letter which I received on Saturday last by the mail. I am very sorry to have so indifferent an account of poor dear Sophy, though I cannot deny that I did not expect to receive a good one. Most anxious do I feel concerning her, and I wish to hear that she is beginning to recover her strength. Till then I shall not feel comfortable, which is very melancholy at the distance I am from her. My last visit at Windsor on the 28th November has, I fear, done her harm. I am very sorry for it, but I really was so much affected at taking leave of her that I could not hide my feelings, and with her delicate frame it is no wonder that she should have suffered from it. Thank God, you can give me a good account of dearest Minny's condition, and I do sincerely hope that she may be rewarded for her courage and angelic patience by a perfect cure.

" My poor friend is, I fear, in a most nervous way. I never can thank you enough for the kind manner in which you write about her, and I recommend her as well as the other two patients to your kind attention, which I have always known to be unremitting indeed to every person without distinction.

" Our beloved king is, thank God, in a happy state for himself, and all one can wish for him *now*, I fear, is that he may remain in it.

"As for myself, I am very tolerably well, considering the hurry and worry I am in. I caught a cold the day after I got on board, and since that I have not been altogether rid of it. The weather here, though very mild for the season, is so damp that I am not surprised at being so long before I get rid of it. I had also lost my sleep, but I am recovering that, and it is no wonder after all I have gone through for this last month. Most heartily do I accept your kind wishes for my success, and would God grant that I may be of use. I assure you that at present my situation is far from agreeable and I am not sleeping on a bed of roses, but I trust when we have got things into some sort of shape I may then be more comfortable.

" Now, my dear Sir Henry, God bless you. Do not forget to write to me when you have time. Remember me to Lady Halford and friend Baillie, and believe me,

" Yours most sincerely,

"ADOLPHUS FREDERICK."

"HANOVER, *October 16th*, 1815.

" I hasten, my dear Sir Henry, to return you my best thanks for your kind letter which I received yesterday, and to assure you that I feel deeply your attention in informing me of the sad operation dearest Minny has been obliged to undergo. Thank God she is well in health, and she writes in excellent spirits, and with her angelic disposition I flatter myself that she will soon get well. She has been sadly plagued with her complaint, but I hope that this last operation will relieve her from any further plague.

" I am grieved to find that the Queen is in your opinion very much weaker ; indeed, at her age it is no wonder after all the worry she has had and which is not yet over, but I hope and trust that her precious life may be preserved for the sake of her family, and particularly of my poor sisters, who would be very much to be pitied indeed if anything was to happen to her at the present moment.

" Dear Sophy is, thank God, wonderfully better. She will, however, I fear be more or less of an invalid, though I trust she may still lead a very different existence than she has done, poor thing, for the last three years of her life.

" You will I am sure do me the justice to believe that I do heartily rejoice at the increase of fortune you have received by the death of Lady Denbigh, and I hope from the bottom of my heart that you and your family may long enjoy it.

" I cannot conclude without mentioning what I know will give you pleasure, that I have enjoyed perfect health ever since I have seen you, and that I really never was better in my life. My time is very much occupied, and I do not see any chance of my paying a visit to my friends in England before next year. Now God bless you, dear Sir Henry, and with my best compliments to Lady Halford, who I hope is well, I remain,

" Yours most sincerely

" ADOLPHUS FREDERICK."

Among the letters from the Duke of Sussex I find the following :

" DEAR SIR HENRY,

" Being anxious to present you with an article which I am sure will be valuable to you as having belonged to my late sister, Princess Augusta, I have now the pleasure of forwarding for your acceptance a clock which the Duchess of Gloucester, the Princess Sophia, and the Duke of Cambridge selected with me from amongst the little treasures of the dear departed. We know that you will prize the trifle, from its having been the property of our beloved sister. And we avail ourselves of this opportunity to express to you our united gratitude for your constant unremitting services, as well as for your faithful and disinterested attachment shown at all times towards every member of the Royal Family, and which has never been more signally evinced than in your indefatigable attendance on our dear sister Augusta. That these are the unanimous sentiments and feelings of every individual of the Royal Family you may rely upon, as also that I esteem myself fortunate in being the organ of such an agreeable communication, and that I am always,

" Dear Sir Henry,
" Your much attached and truly obliged,
" AUGUSTUS FREDERICK."

" KENSINGTON PALACE, *September* 26*th*, 1840.

The following from the Princess Augusta gives an interesting account of an interview with the Emperor of Russia and Grand Duchess and with the King of Prussia :

"Well, Sir Henry, I am alive, and wonderful after the events of this most extraordinary day : after your kind visit, leaving me in my great chair where I intended to remain with my books, &c., about me, conceive about 3 o'clock my receiving a note express from dear Mary saying, 'the E(mperor) is determined with the Gd. Dss. to see you, and my mother says you must receive them as well as you can, and I fear poor Sophy must do the same.'   I sent the note to her, who wisely said the thing was impossible.   I now *rigged* myself and was seated in agony when they announced the Emperor, who received me most graciously, saying everything most obliging, flattering, and so forth, the Gd. Dss. always the same and expressing everything most affectionately: they stayed about half an hour, not quite so much, and I began to breathe, when they brought me a message to say the King of Prussia : this was ten times more, for we were obliged to introduce ourselves to one another ; but talking of the Duchess of York, his brothers, sons, daughters carried me through, and we parted with the greatest civility possible.   I made poor dear Sophy's excuses to the E. and Gd. Dss., assured them she could not see them, for she was in bed ; in short, did all I could to please them, but the fright, hurry, alarm was enough to have undone all your good works.

" I must say all the E. said to me was proper and feeling regarding the P(rince) R(egent).   He talks of staying ten days or a fortnight, and expressed himself enchanted with England hating France, and that he very far from liked his sojourn there.   I make no excuse for this long history ; I have had two notes from Sophy.   I trust her mind will be easier about all this ; she was fussed, but I flatter myself I have spared her everything.

"Frederick called upon her for a moment, which delighted me, as it gave her comfort, and that you well know pleases me. Could you have been behind the curtain, you would have been amused with the scene, tho' from your constant good nature you would have pitied me.

"Very good accounts of the king : all quiet as far as it goes,

"Yours sincerely,

"AUGUSTA.

"*June 10th.*"

There are many letters to Sir Henry Halford from the Princess Mary and the Princess Amelia, in 1810, in reference to the illness and trials of the last named, but they are only of domestic interest. The following letter from the Princess Mary, relates especially to the present then about to be made to Sir Henry, by the several members of the Royal Family, as a mark of friendship and gratitude for his constant kind attentions to the whole of their family. It bears the postmark of August 29th, 1830 :

"MY DEAR SIR HENRY,

"Your letter gave me much pleasure. I am delighted at the conduct of that dear kind-hearted Duke of Cambridge, and I am sure you will be still more gratified when I relate to you what passed between him and me yesterday. I had the pleasure of seeing the Princess Sophia, a few days ago, when I introduced the subject of the *plateau;* she mentioned this to the Duke of Cambridge, and of course we talked the subject over, and he immediately sent to Bridge and Rundell, to know if the models were in existence, and that he was to take them to him this day: one of the plateaus is his late Majesty on foot, and the other on horseback. I am quite for the latter, in which we agreed, as being the handsomest. I understand that the whole of the Royal Family are to subscribe with an inscription to beg your acceptance of it, in all their names as a mark of sincere regard and friendship towards you, and to express the high sense of gratitude they all owe you, for your constant kind attentions to the whole of their family. I told him I had heard from you and he was very anxious to see your letter, which I did not show him, and he desired me to bring it with me to Brighton. I therefore wish, my dear friend, you would write a few lines that I may show him, as I know he would be pleased to hear you approved of the Guelph order, but say nothing about the plateau, as perhaps he may mean it as a surprise. . . .

"God bless you, my dear friend,

"Ever affectionately yours,

"MARY.

"*Thursday morning.*"

From Mrs. Fitzherbert I find the following letters, both without date, but evidently written in 1827, during the illness of the Duke of York :

"MY DEAR SIR HENRY,

"I have made up my mind to go to Brighton on Thursday, provided I am able to do so and that the weather will permit me. I do not like to torment you, but I should be quite unhappy not to see you for a moment before I go. The chief reason of going is that the Pavilion go to town, not to return on the 18th, and I wish to see them, and I shall be thought very ungrateful not to pay my duty, having delayed it so long. If therefore you could any time in the day or evening call, I shall be delighted in person to thank you a thousand times for all your kindness and attention to me, which is deeply impressed upon my heart and mind. Forgive my troubling you, and believe me, with great sincerity,

"Your truly obliged and affectionate

"M. FITZHERBERT.

"TILNEY STREET, *Tuesday evening.*"

"Your letter, my dear Sir Henry, has grieved me to the heart; the account of the poor duke is sad, very sad. I have long thought his case deplorable, but I now begin quite to despair and feel there is no chance of his recovery. Alas! what a loss the country, his family and his friends will sustain. I am sure none will feel or lament it more than I shall.

" The account of his having gone through the operation was publicly talked of here the day after it took place. I mention this for fear you might suppose I had communicated the contents of your letter, not one syllable of which ever passed my lips. I begin to think there is no such thing as a secret in the world.

" What shall I say or how can I express my thanks, my gratitude to you for the trouble you have been so kind, so generous as to take with regard to my papers ? You have no idea of the weight of anxiety and uneasiness you have removed from my mind, for I don't think I should have had a moment's peace or tranquillity had those papers fallen into the hands of those who on a former occasion made such mischief and so many disagreeable scenes and confusion. I really do not know what I should have done, it would have made me miserable. You are very kind in inquiring after me. The waters certainly have done me a great deal of good, but I am sadly tormented with headaches, partly rheumatism. My head at this moment is so confused, I scarcely know what I am about.

" If you should have a moment to spare, and will give me one line to tell me how the duke goes on, you will do me a great favour, for I cannot tell you the anxiety I feel about him. God bless you, my dear and kind friend, for as such I must ever esteem you, and with every good wish to you,

" Believe me always,

" Your very sincere and truly grateful

" M. F."

CHAPTER IX

THE Duke of Wellington was one of Sir Henry Halford's attached friends. The Countess of Mornington, the duke's mother, had been his patient in 1801 ; the duke's brother, the Marquess Wellesley, in 1811. The acquaintance thus formed with the marquess soon grew into friendship which was nurtured by a similarity of tastes —a love of classical literature and of Latin composition. The marquess printed for private distribution in 1840 his " Primitiæ et Reliquiæ," and Sir Henry Halford in 1842 his " Nugæ Metricæ," and each was warmly interested in the work of the other. A frequent correspondence was maintained between them, and from Lord Wellesley's letters I select the following :

"REGENT'S PARK, *February* 18*th*, 1830.

"MY DEAR SIR,

"I return the treatise * with many thanks for the second perusal of it. It is really a very beautiful and interesting composition ; adorned with many fair flowers of Grecian, Roman and English growth. I perceive no addition except Œdipus, with the 'griefless old age' of Theseus.

"I 'burn' is certainly a *verbum ardens ;* but not too ardent for a treatise on the καῦσος. I hope you will choose as good a subject for your next effort.

"Ever, dear Sir, with sincere respect and esteem,

"Your faithful and obliged servant,

"WELLESLEY.

"Sir HENRY HALFORD, Bart."

"MARBLE HILL, *May* 17*th*, 1831.

"MY DEAR SIR HENRY,

"I am greatly obliged to you, for your very interesting publication, which (although I received it only last night) I have read through with very great pleasure.

"The English papers are all extremely well written and composed, and highly interesting. 'Tic Douloureux' throws a new and just light on that most dreadful of all human maladies. 'The Test of Insanity' is very ingenious. The two following papers I have seen before, and I admire them greatly ; the latter especially. I am

* "On the Καῦσος of Aretæus."

not yet quite satisfied with my construction of Γήρως ἄλυπα. I wish you would tell me exactly *how* you construe that phrase.

" The two Latin papers are most admirably and beautifully written ; either I do not understand the language, or they are quite equal to any modern Latin extant. The latter of these papers is extremely interesting.

" I was much pleased with the account of opening the coffin of Charles I. ; the head is very well executed ; and the whole narrative is curious, and affords much matter of solemn reflection.

> ' See what a rent the envious Cromwell made !
> And as he plucked his cursed steel away
> Mark how the blood of England followed it.'

" I was very happy to see Sir Matthew (Tierney), and I have religiously followed his advice and yours. I am recovering slowly from the severity of the influenza ; my other complaint is not worse.

" Believe me always, dear Sir Henry,

" Yours affectionately,

" WELLESLEY."

" HURLINGHAM, *November* 14*th*, 1837.

" MY DEAR SIR HENRY,

" Many thanks for your very valuable present. I have read the Latin verses again and again with great pleasure. Those on

Napoleon are excellent, and the translation from the 'Duenna' very good, and a proof of great power of Latinity.

"I shall study the speeches, I have no doubt, with great benefit. Ever with true regard and gratitude,

"Yours most sincerely,

"WELLESLEY."

Another, very different in character, may be added. Madeira was Sir Henry's favourite wine, that which he habitually drank.

"KINGSTON HOUSE, *February 24th*, 1840.

"MY DEAR SIR HENRY,

"I send you some Madeira. Ever since I left India in 1805, a pipe is sent from the island every year to Bengal, where it remains two years, and then is brought to me. It is usually very fine, and I think this particularly so.

"If you hear anything of Arthur, pray let me know.

"Ever yours sincerely,

"WELLESLEY."

The friendship between Lord Wellesley and Sir Henry Halford, doubtless paved the way to the Duke of Wellington becoming the patient and ere long the warm friend of Sir Henry. The duke in ordinary circumstances was attended by his domestic physician, Dr. Hume, but on all serious occasions Sir Henry was called into consultation.

The duke was in frequent correspondence with Sir Henry Halford. Among the many letters carefully preserved there are the following :

"WOODFIELD, *September* 18*th*, 1826.

" MY DEAR SIR HENRY,

"When I was at Windsor the king spoke to me about going to town to see the Duke of York, which I rather discouraged, as I thought such a visit at this moment might tend to throw the duke back ; and it was not unlikely to affect the king himself a good deal.

"After my conversation with H.M., however, I saw the *Morning Chronicle*, in which there was a paragraph from the Glasgow paper stating the nature of H.R.H.'s disorder and of the remedy which it had been necessary to adopt; and yesterday morning *John Bull* explained the whole case to the public.

"I think now then that it would have an extraordinary appearance, and would become the subject of discussion, if the king were not to pay his brother a visit, and I write to you upon the subject in order to request you to decide, whether this visit (which of course must be repeated occasionally as long as H.R.H. remains within reach of the king and is confined to his house) will be injurious to the duke. If you should think it would be so it must not take place. But if you should think that it would not be injurious to the duke you might then suggest to the King to go and see his brother; or, if you don't like to do so, I will write to his Majesty referring to the opinion which I gave him when I had last the honour of seeing him at Windsor.

" Pray write me a line in answer to this and send it to my house in London, and tell me how H.R.H. is getting on.

" Believe me ever yours most sincerely,

" WELLINGTON."

" LONDON, October 29th, 1826.

" MY DEAR SIR HENRY,

" I return you many thanks for your kindness in writing to me. I have seen your patient [the King], whose appearance I liked very much. He looked better than he has looked for some time, his eyes particularly. But I think he is thin. You have cured him, my dear Sir Henry, and have rendered your country thereby the greatest service, the reflection of which will be some consolation for the pain which you have suffered and the trouble you have taken.

' Believe me ever,

" Yours most sincerely,

" WELLINGTON."

P

The king's illness was now becoming serious, and the following note has reference to the first bulletin that was made public :

"LONDON, *April 27th,* 1830.

" MY DEAR SIR HENRY,

"I have just received your letter, and I have thought it best to have the bulletin published.

"There has been a very general apprehension in respect of the King's health for the last two days, and I am certain that the knowledge of the truth is always the best remedy for such alarms. . . . .

"Believe me, my dear Sir Henry,

"Ever yours most sincerely,

"WELLINGTON."

The physicians in attendance on the King—the signatories of the bulletins—were about this time severely criticised in the public prints, for the character and, as was said, evasiveness of the language employed in them, and which, it was declared,was calculated, if not intended, to mislead. Sir Henry appealed to the Duke of Wellington for advice under the circumstances and received from him the following note :

" LONDON, June 10th, 1830.

" I have received your little note, my dear Sir Henry. You have only to persevere in your own judicious course. Pay no attention to observations from the right or from the left, and you may rely upon it that there is not a good or a judicious man in the country who will not do you justice.

" Believe me, ever yours most sincerely,

" WELLINGTON."

Among many letters of the most friendly nature from the duke, the following is too interesting to be omitted :

" GLOUCESTER LODGE, BAGSHOT PARK,
January 28th, 1834.

" MY DEAR SIR HENRY,

" You will have heard of the great honour about to be conferred upon me by the University of Oxford ; and, knowing as you do, how little qualified I am to fill the situation to which the favour of the university is about to elevate me, you will readily believe that I did everything in my power to prevail upon that body to select one more worthy ; and you will not be surprised at the request which I am about to make to you.

" I understand that the vice-chancellor and certain members of the Convocation are to come to my house on some day between the 3rd and

8th of February, and to announce to me in a Latin oration the honour conferred upon me, and to perform certain ceremonies, to which oration I am to reply in Latin.

" I might not be at a loss to make a suitable reply in English; but as I have scarcely written a line of Latin for nearly half a century, I should be greatly at a loss how to reply in Latin, if I did not reckon upon your facility and classical elegance in writing that language, and your kindness to me upon all occasions.

" I request you then to permit me to send to you as soon as I shall receive it, the purport of the oration of the vice-chancellor which is to be sent to me in writing. I will put down in writing likewise what it occurs to me that I ought to say in reply; and I beg of you to write for me a suitable reply.

" Believe me, my dear Sir Henry

" Ever yours most faithfully,

" WELLINGTON."

The duke's draft of his intended speech, and Sir Henry Halford's Latin version of it, are as follows :

" I was much flattered by the notice taken of me and the honour conferred upon me by the university upon a former occasion; and you have now filled the measure of your confidence and favour by conferring on me the highest and most honourable office which it is in your power to confer, and which associates me with your useful and honourable labours.

"It is impossible for me to express my sense of the honour which you have done me. You do me justice in believing that I am sincerely attached to the ancient laws, constitution and policy of this monarchy; and that I am anxious to maintain a system under the operation of which this country has been raised to the highest pinnacle of prosperity and glory.

"I am sensible of the arduous nature of the duties of the office which you have conferred upon me, as tersely described by the public orator, and of the difficulties of the times in which we live. But, assisted as I hope to be by the advice of some of you, and the concurrence and assistance of all, I hope to be able to co-operate usefully with you and the other public authorities of the university in promoting the objects of your venerable institutions—learning, bonos mores, religion and virtue.

"It will give me the greatest satisfaction to cultivate an acquaintance with the members of the university."

Sir Henry Halford's Latin version is as follows:

INSIGNISSIME VICE-CANCELLARIE,

ILLUSTRISSIMI DOCTORES,

VOSQUE EGREGII PROCURATORES,

Quod me, præclara vestra Universitas Oxoniensis haud indignum judicaverit quem in Cancellarii locum cooptari vellet, etsi tanto honore magnoperè læter, vereor tamen ut studiorum meorum ratio, in omni pæne vitæ decursu, me minùs idoneum saltem, si non ineptum prorsus huic officio reddiderit.

Sed me recreat et reficit pristinæ vestrûm erga me voluntatis recordatio; neque enim me fallet unquam quantâ in illustrium virorum frequentiâ, quantâ in Principum coronâ, me quoque vestris ordinibus adscribi voluistis honoris causâ.

Vester igitur cum jam fuerim, cumque ad summam Academiæ dignitatem vestrum omnium suffragiis evocatus sim, quid rebus vestris præesse morer? Quid vestris institutis atque privilegiis invigilare? Invigilabo iis sedulò, et strenuè ea tuebor.

Vobis sit curæ, disciplinas Academicas longo jam usu comprobatas stabilire et confirmare; doctrinam et literas humaniores fovere; arrectas Juvenum mentes ad virtutem, ad bonos mores, ad religionem, docendo hortandoque, effingere.

Si quid, in his rebus gerendis, concilia mea possint, qua utinam digna essent opinione vestrâ, vobis et Universitati me nunquam defuturum spondeo et polliceor. Eandem enim esse mihi mentem et vobis eadem vota de Ecclesiâ Anglicanâ, de auctoritate Regiâ, de legibus et institutis nostris conservandis et sustinendis, quantum possimus scio. Hæc omnia, ut in perpetuum salva sint faxit Deus optimus Maxumus!!!

The duke submitted his intended speech to a very competent authority, Lord Westmoreland, who wrote, "I think your speech remarkably good Latin, and, without asking further questions, you may compliment the writer for me." The duke expressed to Lord Westmoreland his hope that nobody would ask him whether he wrote it himself.

But it was not in England alone that Sir Henry Halford's opinion or aid in Latin composition was evoked. It was so from the sister island, and by no less than the Primate of all Ireland.

"*May 21st.*

"MY DEAR SIR HENRY,

"I shall be much obliged to you, if you will cast your eye over the within inscription. It is intended to be engraven on the foundation-stone of the tower of our cathedral at Armagh, and to specify the works undertaken in connection with the tower. We wish to be assured that our Latin is free from faults, before we give it to the public.

"Your faithful servant,

"JOHN G. ARMAGH."

The Duke and Duchess of Bedford were among Sir Henry Halford's grateful patients and attached friends. His acquaintance with the

duke began in 1802, when he was called to
Woburn to Francis, the fifth duke, who was then
in extremis and died the 2nd of March 1802.
The first letter I find from the duke is from Dublin
Castle, the 25th of July 1806, in reference to the
actual condition of the great statesman, Mr. Fox :

"PHŒNIX PARK, *July 25th*, 1806.

" MY DEAR SIR,

" My mind is full of anxiety on the state
of Mr. Fox's health, and I hear such various and
contradictory accounts that I cannot be easy till
I learn again from you, what your real opinion is ;
for some days our reports were very sanguine,
since that some of my correspondents give me
every reason to fear the worst, whilst others still
maintain that he continues gradually to amend.
I am persuaded that if there had been any real
amendment such as to hold out a fair prospect of
recovery I should have heard from you ; at all
events let me intreat you to write, as I cannot
bear to be in a state of doubt and uncertainty
upon such a subject.

" If the disorder has made such a progress as
to increase your fears for his life, and to afford
you little or no hope of his valuable days being
spared to us, and he remains still unconscious of
his danger, I think he should not be suffered to
continue so.   No one who knows Mr. Fox can
doubt his fortitude or resignation, and if he knows

his end to be approaching I am sure he will close his life with more satisfaction to himself, by making the remainder of it useful to his country and to those who have unvaryingly considered him as the firmest support of her interests and her happiness,

" Mr. Fox is under no circumstances to be looked upon as an ordinary man.

" I am, dear Sir, with very sincere regard,

"Most faithfully yours,

" BEDFORD."

The next letters are of condolence, on the death of Lady Halford :

"ENDSLEIGH, *Friday*.

" MY DEAR SIR HENRY,

" However much the mind may be prepared for a melancholy event, still the certainty of its having taken place must always be deeply felt. You will therefore excuse my troubling you with a few lines to express that no one ought to feel more sincerely anything that gives you pain than myself, who so often have been indebted to you for the most affectionate attentions, and that as a grateful friend I venture to write to you at this moment, which I hope you will not consider as an intrusion.

" Believe me, my dear Sir Henry,

" Yours truly,

" GEORGINA BEDFORD."

"ENDSLEIGH, *June 22nd*, 1833.

"MY DEAR SIR HENRY,

"I cannot suffer the expression of the duchess's feelings to go to you under my cover, without adding from an old friend, how sincerely I condole with you in the afflicting loss you have sustained.   Your own well-regulated and religious mind will best teach you how to bear this loss.

"I have read the little volume you were good enough to give me on leaving London with infinite delight, and in such a moment the sentiments it breathes cannot fail to be a great consolation to you ; they do equal honour to your head and heart, and although I have not the presumption to say I am a wiser man after I have read these essays, I feel that I am a better man.   I can bear ample testimony to the truth of your opinions from the melancholy experience of my first acquaintance with you in 1802.   You did not deceive me on that occasion, and told me what I was to expect.   When my last hour comes (and it cannot be long delayed) I trust not to be deprived of the consolation of seeing you by my bedside, when I am sure you will administer to me every comfort and every relief, both as a physician and a friend.

"God bless you, my dear Sir Henry, and may He in his infinite mercy long preserve you !

"Truly and affectionately yours,

"BEDFORD."

"Woburn Abbey, *March* 29*th*, 1837.

"My dear Sir Henry,

"I thank you very sincerely for your kind attention. I am used to such acts of kindness and good feeling from you. Lord B. was an excellent, kind-hearted and religious man. Poor Mrs. Fitzherbert too! I had known her well for more than fifty years. She too had a feeling and an excellent heart.

"Always, my dear Sir Henry, with sincere regard and esteem,

"Yours faithfully,

"Bedford."

"Woburn Abbey, *October* 23*rd*, 1837.

"My dear Sir Henry,

"Your kind and friendly letter has met me here on my return from the north. I shall make a point of being in Belgrave Square on Sunday the 29th, unless you will kindly promise to make this your inn on your road to town, and pass one day comfortably with me here. If you can promise me this, I will postpone going to London till the week following. At all events we shall not start to the continent before the second week in November.

"Believe me always, with the truest regard and attachment,

"Faithfully yours,

"Bedford."

"WOBURN ABBEY, *Wednesday morning.*

" DEAR SIR HENRY HALFORD,

"I am delighted at the thought of seeing you here, and of showing you what a good M.D. I am; for the duke has not had one half-hour's illness since we returned to Woburn; his strength is greatly improved; but my chief and grand work has been to convince *his mind* that he is not so ill as at times he thinks, when some indiscretion at table has disordered his stomach. These observations are a complete digression from the design of this note, which is to assure you that we shall be most happy to receive Miss Vaughan with you. Should the day (Friday, 27th) be fine, and that you arrive early, I will take care that you shall both have the means of seeing the gardens, &c. &c., here.

" Believe me, with a grateful remembrance of *thirty-four* years' attention and kindness received upon all occasions, from you, my dear Sir Henry,

"Your sincere and obliged,

"GEORGINA BEDFORD."

"OAKLEY, *October* 29*th*, 1837.

" MY DEAR SIR HENRY,

" I cannot sufficiently thank you for your kind and friendly visit to Woburn, but whilst I have a grateful remembrance of what is so pleasing to my own feelings, I must not forget the sound professional advice of the physician, which I shall endeavour to follow to the utmost of my power, as long as it may please God to spare my life. I am always yours very sincerely, and *thirty-five* years' friendship allows me to add affectionately,

"BEDFORD."

The Duke of Rutland (John Henry, the fifth duke) was among Sir Henry's warmest and fastest friends, and they were often at each other's houses. A similarity of taste and feeling had created and cemented a union between them which only terminated in the death of Sir Henry Halford. The following is an extract from a letter of the duke, dated Belvoir Castle, the 26th of November 1826:

"I am truly anxious to hear of the state of health in which the King finds himself after all the fatigues of the last week. I do not despair of hearing that he thrives on his work and that he is all the better for it. I had a letter from himself on Friday, in which he mentions in terms of the warmest gratitude his sense of the consummate skill and the unwearied and incessant attention and care which *you*, my dear Sir Henry, have evinced towards him in the treatment of his arduous case. I know it will be satisfactory to you to be aware that the pains you have taken are duly appreciated. They are truly appreciated also by a grateful nation.

"Ever, my dear friend,
"Your most sincere and affectionate friend,
"RUTLAND."

"A thousand thanks, dear Sir Henry, for the manner in which you have resumed our correspondence. I can put my hand on my heart and say that no correspondence in which I was ever engaged has given me more satisfaction, no friendship has given more happiness than yours, and I hail the renewal of the former (for the latter never can require renewing), especially under such auspices. . . . . I wrote yesterday to Lord Conyngham to inquire after our gracious sovereign. I rejoice most truly to learn on your authority that he was better yesterday. Whenever you have an opportunity of laying before his Majesty the assurance of my unvarying fidelity and attachment you will greatly oblige,

"My dear friend,
"Yours most faithfully,
"RUTLAND.

"BELVOIR CASTLE, *Jannary* 10*th*, 1828."

The following letter has reference to the sudden death of Sir Henry Halford's youngest brother, the Rev. Edward Vaughan, vicar of St. Martin's, Leicester, whom the duke had met at Wistow but a few days before.

"October 2nd, 1829.

"My dear Sir Henry,

"It is impossible that I can disobey the impulse of my feelings, and I write to say, that after all the instances of sympathetic kindness which I have experienced from you, it would be extraordinary indeed if I did not participate in all that concerns you, whether it be evil or good.

"I deeply lament to find realised the melancholy anticipations which you had formed of the result of your poor brother's illness. He was a man of distinguished science in many points of view, of great importance as a public man, and to his family his life was of the most unutterable consequence. Poor man! who would have thought on hearing him read prayers on the 11th of September (three weeks since this very day) that his valuable life was marked for so early a termination. Scarce a day passes but we see around us that which ought to impress us solemnly and seriously with the fleeting nature of our existence. I will not intrude longer upon you, my sole motive in doing so now being to assure you of the deep sympathy and affectionate interest of,

"My dear Sir Henry,

"Yours ever most faithfully,

"Rutland."

The next letter is on a like subject, the death of Sir Henry's brother, Mr. Justice Vaughan:

"BELVOIR CASTLE, *September 29th*, 1839.

" MY DEAR GOOD FRIEND,

"Can it be that the affliction which I see mentioned in a provincial paper has come upon you and your family, and that your excellent and talented brother, the Chief (*sic*) Justice, has been called away? If I had not known him as I did, and during so long a period of years, my grief on your account and of that of your family would have been most keen. But I have sincerely to grieve on his account also, from the knowledge which I have so long had of his manifold virtues and great excellences. These and your own religious mind will find for you the consolation which can be derived from no other source. I deeply, truly sympathise with you, and I am, in sorrow or in joy, a constant participator in your feelings, and am,

"My dear Sir Henry,

"Your affectionate friend,

"RUTLAND."

"BELVOIR CASTLE, *September 17th*, 1840.

" MY DEAR SIR HENRY,

"Though I have so often troubled you lately, I must give a few lines additional to say with how much gratification I have read your beautiful inscription proposed for the queen's equestrian statue. It is a rare talent, and one to be envied, which enables you to render doubly perfect and interesting such works as the equestrian statue of the queen and the duke.

"I see that you make our Anne unrivalled (as she was) both in peace and war. But she had a powerful assistant for the latter in Marlborough; and mentally I could wish that the 'Dux tuus' of your last line applied to our hero of Waterloo. I rejoice to hear from Lord Bute, who is at Walmer Castle, that the duke is uncommonly well.

"The prolongation of your poor royal patient's suffering (the Princess Augusta), if the final result is no longer doubtful, is questionable as to its desirableness. I never remember a more anxious and harassing case.

"Pray believe me, my dear Sir Henry,
"Your very affectionate friend,
"RUTLAND."

Sir Henry Halford had been long the medical adviser of Sir Robert Peel, and was on terms of most friendly intercourse with him and Lady Peel. Among his letters are the following:

"DRAYTON MANOR, *February 1st.*

"MY DEAR SIR HENRY,

"I return, in compliance with your wish, your very successful translation of the lines from Pope. The last line of Pope is so beautiful and expressive, that I wish it could be the conclusion of the Latin version, particularly as you have the 'lethali transfixus vulnere' in a former line.

The blood oozing out drop by drop and the faint groan are very true to nature. Considering that the stag is dying, would not some epithet be preferable to 'tuta' as an appendix to 'abdita.'

"I shall hope to have the pleasure of keeping my engagement for half-past six, Monday. I will leave Middleton (Lord Jersey's) in time in the morning to enable me to partake of the double feast you have kindly proposed to me.

"My dear Sir Henry,
"Very faithfully yours,
"ROBERT PEEL."

Sir Henry accepts his friend's suggestion, and the lines, as altered, are as follow :

"Sic modò lethali transfixus arundine cervus
Sylvarum latebras, et loca tecta petit :
Ille inter gemitus miser et suspiria, tardâ
Guttatim effuso sanguine morte perit."*

The following friendly letter from the same distinguished source may be added :

"DRAYTON MANOR, *August* 19*th.*

"MY DEAR SIR HENRY,
"We rejoice to hear of your return, partly from the selfish hope that we can prevail on you

---

* I add, for facility of comparison, Pope's original :

"So the struck deer in some sequester'd part
Lies down to die—the arrow at his heart ;
He stretch'd unseen, in coverts hid from day,
Bleeds drop by drop, and pants his life away."

again to order your horses for a morning's drive (for remember, it is no more), and repeat your visit to Drayton Manor. In the words of one of the worst lines in Ovid,

'Nil mihi rescribas attamen ipse veni.'

"I shall, however, be entirely reconciled to the line—even to the 'attamen'—if you will accede to the prayer it conveys, and make your appearance here without the delay even of previous notice. Your bed will be ready, and you cannot doubt of the hearty welcome with which you will be received.

"Sir James Scarlett left us yesterday morning, having slept here on his way from Gloucester to Lancaster, with his head, and his pockets too, full of special retainers. He passed through Cheltenham, but at too early an hour to call on the Duke of Gloucester.

"I am desired by Lady Peel to send you her kindest regards, and to tell you that her sister Lady Fuller is here, and that if you will come before Monday next (when the Fullers probably leave us) you will be received with general rejoicing.

"Ever, my dear Sir Henry,

"Most faithfully yours,

"ROBERT PEEL."

The following letters are from an accomplished patient and friend, the Hon. General Phipps :

"MOUNT STREET, *Saturday morning, July* 14*th*, 1832.

"MY DEAR SIR HENRY,

"I hasten to thank you for the very interesting book you have had the kindness to send me, and which I found on my breakfast-table this morning. I have dipped into it, and met with your eulogy on the late Dr. Warren, which is much more applicable to yourself: 'Tantam denique morum comitatem et facilitatem (habes) ut nemo (te) semel usus esset medico, quin socium voluerit et amicum.' I can bear testimony to the justness of the application.

"Your account of what appeared on opening the coffin of King Charles the First I was particularly desirous of having, and am glad to find it in the work I have before me, for which I beg to repeat my thanks. I have the honour to be,

"My dear Sir Henry,

"Very truly yours,

"EDM. PHIPPS."

"MOUNT STREET, *April* 14*th*, 1835.

"MY DEAR SIR HENRY,

"I deferred writing to thank you for the book you were so good as to favour me with until I had read it, that I might tell you how much I like it. I am delighted with it, and was pleased to see your defence of Cardinal Wolsey, whom all good scholars should defend for the service he rendered to literature. You are 'a Griffith' to him, and those who read what you have written of the Cardinal will be as much affected by it as Queen Katherine was by what Griffith said of him.

"What you say of Edward the Sixth was exemplified in a brother of mine, I have been told, who died when I was too young to know him. Your concluding sentence upon this subject reminds me of what Velleius Paterculus said of Servilia, 'Lepidi uxor quæ prematuram mortem immortali nominis sui pensavit memoriâ.'

"You have shown up Bishop Burnet in his proper colours, bigoted and illiberal; the tenets of the Protestant Church which he professed should have taught him more justice, liberality and Christian charity. He was too dogmatical upon the case of Queen Mary, a subject he did not understand, in his censure of Dr. Radcliffe, a physician of the highest reputation. The bishop by over-zeal does injustice to himself, who possessed much learning and piety.

"You have acted kindly by Dean Swift in showing that he was censured for what was his misfortune, not his fault; as Churchill says, 'and find that nature's errors are my own.' I hope when the dinners at Lambeth are renewed we shall meet there and sit together again.

> 'Hic dies verè mihi festus atras
> Eximet curas,'

which O'Connell causes, since our Cæsar Peel has

been obliged to yield to him.   I hope, however, it will be only a retreat, not a defeat.

"Believe me, my dear Sir Henry, with the greatest regard,

"Sincerely yours,

" E. Phipps."

" Mount Street, August 19th, 1835.

" Dear Sir Henry,

"I hear you were to return to town yesterday, which I am glad of, as there is no doing without you.   About a month ago I had a bilious attack, and knowing you were out of town I sent to Dr. Hume in your neighbourhood, and he, as if you had dropped 'your mantle' on him; made me well in two days.   I had another attack since, when he also was out of town.   I then had recourse to my old friend, Baume de Vie, which also made me soon well.

"I should not have troubled you with this detail had I not wished for an excuse to write and tell you I found on looking over some old family papers a copy of verses in my father's hand-writing, describing the merits of the eminent physicians of his day; and as it appeared to me that all their merits are combined in you, I altered them so as to apply to you, and beg to present them as an offering to my ' Magnus Apollo.'

"Believe me, my dear Sir Henry,

" Very truly yours,

" E. Phipps."

To Sir Henry Halford, Bart., M.D., G.C.H., &c. &c.

> "Halford, well skilled in medicine, imparts
> His healing aid, and captivates our hearts,
> His gentle manners, science, and address
> Render our fancied ills and real less.
>
>   *   *   *   *   *
>
> Curious yet cautious, daring yet discreet,
> None for the chair of president so meet,
> As he who now in practice takes the lead
> As erst did Radcliffe, Arbuthnot and Mead.
>
> *August* 1835."

In the following letter from Lord Grosvenor, there is a graceful recognition of Sir Henry Halford's classical attainments:

> "Motcombe House, Shaftesbury,
> *August* 14*th*, 1839.

" My dear Sir Henry,

"Your great kindness in sending me the graceful translation of the beautiful lines of Goldsmith has not received a fitting acknowledgment, but it is not that it has fallen into ungrateful hands. When you were so kind as to repeat them to me I did not venture to ask for a copy, but now that I have been so fortunate as to obtain it, I have made to me a very important use of it, not only by putting it into my children's hands to learn, but also by laying before them the bright example of the exalted species of relaxation resorted to by one who has been subjected to the daily and nightly harass of a laborious profession, entering at the same time with interest into the refinements of social life.

"From your long intimacy with my poor mother-in-law, the late Duchess of Sutherland, I think you will read with some interest the lines which accompany this; from the reference made in them to her and from their having, I think, merit as a composition. You will run over them too with pleasure as the production of my brother-in-law, and from the just tribute they pay to the kind and amiable man whose loss they deplore.

"Believe me, my dear Sir Henry, with best remembrances from Lady Grosvenor,

"Most sincerely yours,

" GROSVENOR."

The following from his friend Colonel Grosvenor, another member of the same family, is amusing :

" UPPER HALL PARK.

" MY DEAR SIR HENRY,

"I am still basking in the sunshine that always irradiates you.

"It was a most pleasant circumstance the meeting you at our friend the duke's. A glimpse of the sun is better than nothing. I could have wished it could have shone with a full refulgence for four-and-twenty hours on my little domain.

How time slips away! I may say it is a slippery age, or rather that our age is of a sliding nature.

"I cannot guess with any certainty what year it was when I passed three or four days so pleasantly and agreeably under your hospitable roof in Leicestershire. I came not *alone*, as you remember. But I will say no more on that head. You know what I might say.

"But, thank God, my stars have been lucky stars. And to go back to the 'Orb of Day,' if you, Sir Henry, ever bless us with your sunshine on this little spot of my own creation you will find in a *second* mate of mine a heart and disposition to appreciate your virtues and the kindly feeling and friendship that has so long characterised our acquaintance.

"I have ordered my groom to parade before you the chestnut filly foal (by Vanish) which I mentioned to you this morning. She will be in the duke's courtyard when you get into your chaise. If you are disposed to pay me the compliment of accepting her, you will be doing me a pleasure, and it will be a kind of link of adhesion in the long chain of my regard towards you.

"Believe me, my dear Sir Henry,

"Ever most truly and attached, yours,

"T. GROSVENOR."

In the following, from Lord Holland, there is a pleasing testimony to the worth of the Duke of

York, which, coming from a political opponent, is the more valuable.

"DEAR SIR HENRY,

"I congratulate you from my heart on the amendment of the Duke of York so much beyond expectation, and I hope there is now a reasonable hope of recovery. There never was a more sincere and general wish for the recovery of one of his rank, in all parties, and full as strong among those who differ, as among those who agree with him in politics—a gratifying and a just reward this—for there never was a man who kept more religiously the fair distinction between political distinction and personal enmity than he has always done, and I now hope will long continue to do.

"Yours truly,

"VASSALL HOLLAND."

In a postscript he adds:

"The Duke of Bedford is wonderfully well—another of your miracles. You outdo all the Hohenlohes in the world."

The following is from the Duke of Dorset:

"DRAYTON HOUSE,
Friday, September 23rd, 1831.

"MY DEAR SIR HENRY,

"I beg to assure you that nothing would have given me greater pleasure than paying my respects to you at Wistow, and having the opportunity of expressing my thanks to you personally for your very great kindness to us all. My poor brother has suffered much (as you well know) and his spirits were of course affected by the prospect of still greater inflictions. I wish you could have witnessed (for I am sure it would have gratified you) the sudden effect produced by your answer to Mr. Leete's letter on Saturday last. The implicit confidence my brother felt in your opinion restored his mind to tranquillity instantaneously, and from that moment his amendment has been progressive. To express my gratitude towards you would be impossible, but I am sure you will give me credit for appreciating your kindness as it so well deserves.

"Believe me, my dear Sir Henry, with sincere regard,

"Most truly and gratefully yours,

"DORSET."

The two following letters from the Duke of Cleveland are of or about this date. The first of them "enclosed a draft for £500 for a journey to Newton House, near Bedale, Yorkshire, 224 miles from London."

"NEWTON HOUSE, *Saturday night.*"

"MY DEAR FRIEND,

"No trifling pecuniary remembrance

can at all satisfy the obligation that I feel due to you for your prompt and gratifying attention to the wishes of Lady C. and myself, which I shall ever hold in most grateful recollection.

" Should the enclosed be inadequate to the many losses you may sustain by absence, scruple not to name it to me and impute it to my ignorance.

" Ever, my dear Sir,

" Very faithfully yours,

" CLEVELAND.

" NEWTON HOUSE, December 5th, Friday.

" MY DEAR SIR HENRY,

" I am doubly gratified by the receipt of your very kind letter this morning, first because you were relieved on your arrival from your anxiety, and secondly that you had not personally suffered from the rapidity of your long journey and your successful exertions in administering benefit and comfort to myself and Lady Cleveland, which you succeeded in doing to the greatest extent, and which merited more than any token I could offer of my gratification.

" I have been on horseback three days, but have had resolution not to hunt till Monday next. I have no remains of illness (although all the newspapers have killed me) except weakness in my instep and soles of my feet.

" I was truly rejoiced at the good account you gave me of his Majesty, and much flattered by his notice of me.   Lady Cleveland charges me to offer you her kindest wishes.

" Believe me, my dear Sir Henry,

" Yours very sincerely,

" CLEVELAND."

The following letter of the elder D'Israeli to his friend and physician, Dr. Gordon of Finsbury Square, is interesting, and the more so as Mr. D'Israeli was thought to be reserved and scrupulous in his award of praise to any one.   The letter has reference to the inquiries which Sir Henry Halford was making in preparation of his essay, " On the Deaths of some Eminent Persons of Modern Times " :

" BRADENHAM HOUSE, WEST WYCOMBE,
October 1st, 1836.

" MY DEAR SIR,

" Of Dr. Bate's ' History of the last sickness of the Protector,' I do not immediately recollect any other than what appears in this physician's narrative of the troubles in England published in Latin under the title of ' Elenchus Motuum Nuperorum in Anglia, &c.'   In the second part will be found some account of the Protector's malady, and the opening of the body. Whether the particulars there given will prove satisfactory, it is not for me to judge.

" Let me further observe that there are several editions of this work.   I imagine that the best is that of 1663, 8vo.   I do not consider the book rare.

" I do not recollect that Dr. Bate's account of 'the last sickness of Cromwell' was ever separately published; and I conclude that we have no other than what may be found in his history.   I am surprised that Sir Henry Ellis should not have readily reminded Sir Henry Halford of Bate's volume as the most likely to contain the desired information, conversant as both these gentlemen are with the history of that interesting period,

" It was rumoured at the time that the Protector had been poisoned.   Whitelock has chronicled it, and the friends of Dr. Bate humoured the report, insinuating that this political stroke, the stroke of death, came from the assassinating hand of the physician !—anything served to recommend the principal physician of Cromwell to the same station under the new sovereign ; and the doctor seemed equally skilled in administering his strong doses to his Highness the Protector, or his sacred Majesty.

" I am highly gratified to learn that my commentaries on the reign of Charles the First are honoured with the approbation of so competent a judge as Sir Henry Halford ; the commendation of such men is the only reward of my labours that I value.

"Sir Henry Halford indeed has a particular claim on my attention. I have long been delighted by his beautiful discourses. Unlike the vague and generalising philosophers of this day, he builds on the firm foundation of collected facts and deduces from his demonstrations, with much refined taste, so many novel truths.

"Believe me, with regards, my dear Sir,

"Faithfully yours,

"I. D'ISRAELI.

"Dr. J. A. GORDON."

The following letter will interest my medical readers. It is from Sir Henry Halford to Sir Charles (then Mr.) Bell, in acknowledgment of a copy of his celebrated paper on the nerves, which appeared in the Philosophical Transactions of 1821:

"MY DEAR SIR,

"I found your paper on my table when I returned to town on Friday evening, and, having read it carefully, I thank you for it with more than usual earnestness.

"You have opened a field of knowledge to the profession at large, and of fame to yourself, I trust, from whence the fullest harvest must be gathered. Go on, and prosecute the discovery which you have made throughout the whole system of nerves, and I am sure the profession at large will owe you a great debt.   Let me assure you of my sense of the value of your labours, and depend upon me for availing myself of every occasion of expressing and manifesting it.

"I am, with great regard, yours,

"My dear Sir, truly,

"HENRY HALFORD.

"CURZON STREET, *November 4th*, 1821."

Sir Henry was a warm admirer of Sir Charles Bell, and fully appreciated his labours and discoveries in the anatomy and physiology of the nerves.   It was Sir Henry Halford who wrote the inscription engraved on the piece of silver plate presented to Sir Charles Bell, by his friends and admirers, in 1836, when he finally left London for Edinburgh.

Henry Halford

CHAPTER X

Sir Henry Halford was below the middle stature. He was of sanguine temperament, light complexion and had blue eyes, with a kind and intelligent expression of countenance and pleasing, polished manners. His hair, until it turned white, was powdered, his whiskers small, and he was close shaved to a level with the ears. He wore a deep white cravat and a full-frilled shirt. His outer attire was entirely of black ; a dress-coat buttoned high across the breast, a black waistcoat, and breeches, fastened at the knee with a buckle; black silk stockings, and shoes either tied with ribbon or fastened with a silver buckle. Towards the end of his life he wore black trousers. This, or something akin to it, was the correct dress of a physician at the end of the last and the beginning of the present century.

Sir Henry Halford's portrait, by Sir Thomas

R

Lawrence, is at Wistow. It was engraved by C. Turner, A.R.A. There is a good likeness of him in 1837, drawn by H. Room for Pettigrew's Medical Portrait Gallery, and engraved by Cochran. His bust by Chantrey, in 1825, is in the Censor's Room of the College of Physicians.

Sir Henry Halford had been gifted with a clear perception, a sound judgment and a retentive ready memory. He saw his object at once, and with intuitive sagacity saw it clearly and in its true relations. He had too, in a very marked degree, the power of fixing his attention on the subject before him, to the exclusion of other thought, or of distractions of any kind, and he habitually cultivated this faculty in all circumstances. Nothing is more important than this habit of fixed attention. It is only acquired at an early period of life, when habits are most easily established, and Sir Henry is said to have been noted for it even as a boy at Rugby. These qualities of mind had been disciplined and improved by his education at a public school, and by the complete course of studies he went through at Oxford.

His tendency in all things was to the practical and useful, not to the speculative or theoretical ; a fact which comes out strongly in his notes of the lectures he attended at Edinburgh.

Soon after Sir Henry settled in London he became known to the first Dr. Warren, then the leading and most popular physician in town. There was something very similar in their respective characters, and they would seem to have taken mutually to one another. Dr. Warren predicted that his young friend would rise to the head of his profession ; and Sir Henry always spoke of Dr. Warren as the nearest approach he had met with, to that ideal of a perfect physician which he had formed in his own mind. He took Dr. Warren for his own model, and fashioned himself as nearly as he could to that distinguished physician. How well he succeeded is evident from this, that had he, twenty years later on, when at the zenith of his own reputation, been called on to portray himself and his own professional characteristics, he could not have done it better than in the very words he used in his Harveian oration of 1800, to set forth the character and excellences of his prototype, Dr. Warren. I give in a note this sketch of Dr. Warren.* Its applicability to himself, will be evident as we proceed.

* "Ecquis erat unquam scientiâ morborum locupletatus magis, vel magis curatione exercitatus ; ecquis erat unquam qui suavi illâ sermonis et morum humanitate, quæ in ipso

Sir Henry Halford, like his prototype, was essentially a practical bedside physician—an accurate and judicious observer, who knew what remedies can and what they cannot accomplish.   He had a wide and accurate knowledge of the action and

remediorum loco haberi potest, ecquis erat unquam qui Warrenum superabat?   Erat illi ingenii vis maxuma, perceptio et comprehensio celerrima, judicium acre, memoria perceptorum tenacissima.   Meministis, Socii, quam subtiliter, et uno quasi intuitu res omnes ægrotantium perspiceret penitùs et intelligeret! in interrogando quam aptus esset et opportunus, quam promptus in expediendo!   Omnia etenim artis subsidia statim illi in mentem veniebant, et nihil ei novum, nihil inauditum videbatur.   In ea autem facultate quâ consolamur afflictos, et deducimus perterritos a timore, quâ languidos incitamus et erigimus depressos, omnium Medicorum facilè princeps fuit; et si qui medicamentis non cessissent dolores, permulcebat eos, et consopiebat hortationibus et alloquio.

> ' stetit urna paulùm
> Sicca, dum grato Danai puellas
> Carmine mulcet.'

Verum ea est quodammodo artis nostræ conditio, ut Medicus, quamvis sit eruditus, quamvis sit acer et acutus in cogitando, quamvis sit ad præcipiendum expeditus, si fuerit idem in moribus ac voluntatibus civium suorum hospes, parum ei proderit oleum operamque inter calamos et scrinia consumpsisse.   Warrenus autem in omni vitæ et studiorum decursu, si quis unquam alius, Pallade dextrâ usus est, atque omnium qùibuscum rem agebat mentes sensusque gustavit; et quid sentirent, quid vellent, quid opinarentur, quid exspectarent arripuit, percepit, novit.   Tantum denique morum comitatem et facilitatem habuit, ut nemo eo semel usus esset Medico, quin socium voluerit et amicum." (Oratio ex Harveii Instituto, habita die Octob. xviii.   Anno MDCCC.)

powers of drugs and of the other appliances of his art, and employed them with a confidence and success which afforded full proof of his sagacity and their correctness. Much of his knowledge on these points he would seem to have derived from his father.

He had great confidence in the power of nature to cure disease—in the *vis medicatrix naturæ*—and held that nature, although powerful, was obsequious and might be aided in her efforts or thwarted by the physician. Like all wise physicians he treated the *vis medicatrix*, as the sunflower does the sun—he followed it until it became invisible.

Sir Henry was keenly alive to the influence of mind upon the body and its diseases, especially so to the power of hope in aiding, and of fear in opposing, nature's most salutary efforts.

> " Our greatest good and what we least can spare
> Is hope : the last of all our evils, fear."

All the depressing passions of the mind are injurious to disease. By disturbing the curative efforts of nature, they interfere with the normal course of disease, and they weaken or neutralise the operations of the *vis medicatrix*. Grief, anxiety and care were, in Sir Henry Halford's experience, only second to fear in their baneful influence on bodily disease, and on the recuperative powers innate in the human frame, and they received from him an equal amount of consideration in his treatment and care of the sick.

Confidence in the physician is said to be half the cure,* because it keeps up hope and lends to the body the support of the mind. But when despair co-operates with the disease, they react upon one another, and a curable complaint is converted into a mortal one. The expectation of the event has here a share in producing it, for a slight shock completes the destruction of energies already prostrate.

Sir Henry Halford is said to have ministered to symptoms rather than to the disease, of which symptoms are the consequence and the exponent. But an examination of his case-books and prescriptions, of which there are many at Wistow, satisfies me that he did so only, in as far as was compatible with a due consideration and treatment of the disease itself. We all do so more or less, and rightly, for the comfort of our patients; but Sir Henry did it more freely, and it must be conceded more effectually, than many of his contem-

* "Plus interdum prodesse fiduciam in Medicum quam ipsam medicinam."—AVICENNA.

poraries. He had fully realised that disease runs a definite course, which cannot be advantageously altered. It may be too, that he did not wholly dissent from the Spanish Benedictine, Feijoo, that "medicine can seldom do more than remedy the symptoms or effects of the disease, but the essence of it remains unmoved till nature alone overcomes it." *

Sir Henry was solicitous in all cases to allay or ease pain, to ensure rest and a due amount of sleep at night, and to maintain the appetite for food, and support the power and functions of the stomach. These objects he kept steadily in view, and wisely so, as those who have had extensive experience in private practice will be the first to admit. It was owing probably to his marked attention to these three circumstances, and his rule in all cases of ministering to them such aid as medicines could supply, that the charge against him of prescribing for mere symptoms originated. I have stated before and now repeat, that he did it as complementary to, and not in place of, active and efficient treatment of the disease itself. But here I would make the remark that the older the physician and the larger his experience, the more

* "On the Uncertainties in the Practice of Physick." 12mo, London, 1751, p. 4.

does he prescribe for symptoms.   Such is my own individual tendency, as it is of contemporaries of my own age and experience, in the actual practice of physic.

Sir Henry is reported to have had a remedy, and for the most part a temporarily efficient one, for most of the pains and other sufferings to which man is subject, and he administered them with a success which impressed his patients with surprise and gratitude.   Unfortunately, and to the loss of the art of medicine, the knowledge of many of these has perished with him.   They were not recorded as they should have been in his lifetime, or when still fresh in the recollection of his contemporaries, and it is now too late to recover them.

He was by nature sanguine, and was hopeful under almost all circumstances.   It was a principle with him, to take the most favourable view he could truthfully and honestly do of the disease and condition of his patient, and he had the faculty in a somewhat remarkable degree of imparting the like feeling to others, and particularly to the patient himself.

He had too an innate shrinking from bodily pain and from grief or suffering of any kind, and he spared nothing in his efforts to remove or assuage them. His solicitude for his patients, and his oft-avowed principle of interposing himself between the sufferer and everything which could possibly aggravate his sufferings or increase his danger, are beyond all praise. This was in part the secret of the unbounded trust and confidence he inspired in his patients. A lady of the highest rank is reported to have declared she would rather die under Sir Henry Halford's care than recover under any other physician. This remark is only quoted in proof of the extraordinary influence he exerted over those who came under his professional care.

Coleridge tells us in his "Table Talk" that in the treatment of nervous diseases he is the best physician who is the most ingenious inspirer of hope. Sir Henry Halford's experience had taught him to regard hope as of wider, indeed of very general application in the treatment of disease wheresoever situated, and as we have seen in previous pages he acted on that conviction. It may be thought—it was thought by some of his contemporaries—that he sometimes urged this principle to its extremest limits, as in the cases of the Duke of York and George IV. I am myself disposed to think that he did so. But this is one of the most difficult and delicate questions in medical ethics, and must not be argued here. I have considered it at some length in a little book, " Euthanasia," * to which I may refer my readers.

Sir Henry by his sympathy, his gentleness of manner and the hope he inspired, often did for his patient more than any drugs could effect, and when all these failed to bring relief and the malady was beyond the reach of his skill, the minds of the sick were consoled by his conversation, and their cares, anxieties and fears soothed by his presence.

> " Sunt verba et voces quibus hunc lenire dolorem
> Possis, et magnam morbi deponere partem."

He had too, in a marked degree, the faculty of transforming patients into admiring and grateful friends. Of this I have given abundant proof in previous pages. Whether this in a worldly and professional point of view be a desirable faculty is not so certain. Sir Thomas Watson, the most distinguished of all who have succeeded Sir Henry Halford in the presidency of the College of Physicians, was doubtful if it really was so.

Sir Henry Halford is said to have been

* " Euthanasia : or Medical Treatment in aid of an easy Natural Death." 12mo, London, 1887. Longmans & Co.

imperious in the sick chamber, not to his patient, to whom he was all sympathy, kindness and gentleness, but to the attendants and to all who were admitted into the room. So much do the comfort and well-being of the sick depend on the bearing of those around them, that within due limits he was doubtless right.

The patient and his needs having been duly cared for, and his surroundings in the sick chamber fittingly regulated, Sir Henry's next thought was of the family of the patient, who in doubtful and especially in serious cases need whatsoever consolation the physician can justly and truthfully impart, to assuage their apprehensions and anxiety.

To sum up. Sir Henry Halford's attainments as a practical physician were of the highest order. Although, perhaps, as was said, inferior to his great contemporary and friend Dr. Baillie in minuteness of diagnosis, he was undoubtedly superior to him in that which constitutes the real aim and office of the physician—the cure and alleviation of disease.* In this point of view Sir

* A distinguished contemporary physician, Dr. Marshall Hall, who knew Dr. Baillie and Sir Henry Halford, and had frequently met the last named of them in consultation, writes : " Dr. Baillie, remarkable for his skill in the detection of

Henry Halford attained to consummate skill. Endowed, as has been said, with quick perception, a sound judgment and an almost intuitive knowledge of the powers of medicines, he wielded the resources of his art with a confidence, precision and success which was unapproached by any of his contemporaries.

A distinguished surgical contemporary of Sir Henry Halford, Sir Benjamin Brodie, states in his " Autobiography," but as I contend incorrectly, that Sir Henry Halford, although a clever and sagacious physician with a great deal of practical information, was without any of that scientific knowledge which is necessary for a right diagnosis of disease.

A scientific knowledge of medicine is understood to imply a knowledge of the sciences on which the art of medicine is founded—of

diseases, proposed but scanty resources for their treatment ; while Sir Henry Halford, less able perhaps in diagnosis, was remarkable for his fertility and invention in regard to remedies. This fertility in resources," continues he, "is not, perhaps, the highest or most scientific branch of medicine ; but it is indubitably that which, if judiciously applied in practice, affords the greatest solace and benefit to the patient, and may therefore be regarded as the highest faculty which a physician can possess in the actual exercise of his art. Like all other faculties, it may be greatly augmented by exercise." It was so with Sir Henry Halford.

anatomy, physiology, chemistry, pathology, &c.—
to each of which subjects Sir Henry Halford had
applied closely and successfully at Edinburgh,
where, at the period referred to, they were more
completely and better taught than anywhere else
in these kingdoms. His notes of the lectures he
attended at Edinburgh are full, and show how
diligently he studied and mastered them.

I know of no one of Sir Henry Halford's
contemporaries who, at the time of commencing
practice, was better instructed than he, not in one
subject only, but in all of those that go to make
up the science of medicine. His early success
in practice left him no leisure to keep himself
on a level with all the advances that were then
being made in each of these subjects, nor indeed
for further special cultivation of them. But he
kept himself abreast with all the great discoveries
and improvements in the science and art of physic
that were made in his time.

He was an earnest and consistent advocate of
vaccination from its introduction by Dr. Jenner
in 1798 to his own death in 1844.* He was too
amongst the first to recognise the truth and
value of Sir Charles Bell's great discovery of the
functions and structure of the spinal nerves.† Sir

* *Ante*, p. 50.   *Ante*, p. 254.

Henry accepted, at once and unreservedly, the teachings of Dr. Prout on urinary pathology and animal chemistry; and although he never learned to practise auscultation—for his age and many engagements were insuperable obstacles to his mastering its many difficulties—he saw and admitted the aid that was to be derived from the stethoscope in the diagnosis of disease. In 1826 Dr. Scudamore requested permission to dedicate to Sir Henry Halford, a brochure on " Laennec's Diagnosis of Diseases of the Chest by the Stethoscope and Percussion," and this led to the following letter :

" MY DEAR DR. SCUDAMORE,

"I had written some remarks, but I think it better to ask you to give me the opportunity of talking with you for five minutes. I am much pleased and flattered by your kind attention, and if you will introduce your subject with three or four sentences expressive of your sense of the propriety of ascertaining diseases rather by the symptoms which accompany them than by mechanical examination—though in the present imperfect state of our knowledge on various points, no prudent physician will disdain the subsidiary aid even of instruments to give him a more correct insight into what is going on—if you will do this, I say, I shall be proud of your dedication, and I believe it will contribute materially to make the pamphlet acceptable, and the use of the stethoscope practised. . . . ."

> "With great regard,
>
> "Your faithful friend,
>
> "HENRY HALFORD.

"*Sunday.*"

The tendency of Sir Henry Halford's mind indisposed him to whatever was not essentially and immediately practical. The prevention and cure of disease and the alleviation of suffering are the essential objects of the medical art, and the physician should not allow anything to divert his attention from them. The study of disease at the bedside and of all the resources of his art—of diet, medicines, and other appliances, curative and palliative—were what henceforth especially engaged Sir Henry's attention and made him the successful practitioner he was acknowledged to be by all his contemporaries.

He was always careful to give due attention to each subject, but not to cultivate any one of them to the prejudice of the others. He himself, when at the summit of his reputation, and speaking on the education of a physician, says, "To become exclusively the botanist or chemist, or even the anatomist, where the one great object is the cure of diseases, will narrow both his resources and his mind, and make him incur the risk of failure in the end. THE CURE OF DISEASES IS THE PHYSICIAN'S OBJECT, AND HE MUST NOT ALLOW ANYTHING TO DIVERT HIS EYE FROM THAT GREAT MARK."

As respects Sir Henry Halford's powers of diagnosing disease, which were questioned by Sir Benjamin Brodie, I would observe that Dr. Hawkins, who knew Sir Henry so well, describes him "ad morbos dijudicandos sagax." And the case of the Duchess of Devonshire, in which Sir Henry of all the physicians in attendance, and Dr. Baillie was one of them, alone formed a correct diagnosis, is in evidence to the same effect.

But Sir Benjamin Brodie is constrained after all to admit, that Sir Henry Halford was a clever and sagacious physician, with a great deal of practical information, and was on the whole a very useful and successful practitioner, in many respects an ornament of his profession, and a worthy representative of it, as president of the College of Physicians.

The same critic says of Sir Henry Halford, " He was a good Latin scholar, and prided himself rather over-much on his skill in composing

Latin verses." On this passage I am not disposed to say much. Skill in composing Latin verses is, at any rate, the token of a good scholar, and to have been fond of it, is at most an amiable weakness. Besides, as we are taught by Keble, poetry is a method of relieving an overburdened mind; and is a channel through which emotion finds a safe and regulated expression. There are few who can prefer a better claim to such a resource, than one so fully engaged as was Sir Henry Halford, in all the anxieties of medical practice.

During Sir Henry Halford's time, a good knowledge of the Latin language was considered one of the necessary attainments of a physician; to neglect, undervalue and disparage it, does not even now conduce to keep up the dignity of the medical profession in its higher ranks. It was a taste he shared with statesmen and men in high places, as his correspondence sufficiently attests. The classics throughout the whole of Sir Henry Halford's life were indeed his amusement and resource from the monotony and weariness of professional work, and especially Latin composition and Latin poetry in which he was a proficient; and for which he was noted among the elegant scholars of his time. He spoke Latin with ease and elegance—an important attainment for a president of the College of Physicians at a time when the examinations of candidates for the diploma of the college were conducted wholly or in part in that language.

Sir Henry Halford was fond of society, and shone in it. He was given to anecdote, and to speaking of those interesting incidents of which he was specially cognisant, and of those in which he had been called upon to take part. Hence probably the statement of one of his friends, Miss Williams-Wynn,* that he was apt to be the hero of his own stories. But he was careful not to make his own share in conversation unduly prominent. He was a good, an attentive listener; and he only interposed when an opening invited him to do so, or the conversation flagged. He is said to have been specially happy in his talk on classical subjects, then a much more frequent topic of conversation among men than now.

He was an excellent host, especially at Wistow, where he was free from the anxieties and distractions of medical practice, and was able to devote himself to all the duties and amenities of

* "Diaries of a Lady of Quality," edited by A. Hayward, Q.C. London, 1864, p. 215.

social life. That he did so, liberally and almost regardless of expense, is certain.

It was an axiom with Sir Henry Halford that it is better to live rich than to die rich (they are his own words), and he seems to have acted up to it from a very early period of his professional life. Notwithstanding his very large professional income for so long a series of years, he left but little behind him save the Wistow estate, which, however, he had got into very good condition, and to which he had largely added. In the letter of March, 1823, before referred to (page 65), after specifying his outlay on Wistow, he says: " This accounts for all the savings of my professional laborious life, and as it amounts to nearly £70,000, I do not feel ashamed that after so large a measure of success I have not husbanded a greater saving, considering that I have never denied my family one luxury which it was possible for them to enjoy. All these savings are gone to make Wistow productive at all." He speaks too, of looking forward at this time (1823) to " a material abridgment of expense by no more farmhouses requiring to be built." But abridgment of his ordinary current expenses did not then come.

From an early period of Sir Henry's married life he had been in the habit, on his return home in the evening from his professional rounds, of emptying his pockets of the whole of his daily earnings into his wife's lap, and of leaving it in her keeping and to her management. Indeed, Lady Halford, up to her last illness, managed Sir Henry's money matters so far as they were managed, for he himself seems to have been almost helpless in these respects, or too much occupied to attend to them. For some time after Lady Halford's death, they were left almost to take care of themselves. The result was that he was plundered without stint or mercy by some of his domestics, and his expenses in Curzon Street and at Wistow, but particularly at Curzon Street, had become so large as to be a ground for serious apprehension and of some present embarrassment ; until one of his nieces went to reside with him, who at once reduced the establishment and so curtailed his expenditure.

Sir Henry did with little sleep. He retired late and rose early. Most of his correspondence, and it was extensive, was done at night. Every morning when the weather permitted he walked, or preferably rode on horseback, in the park for an hour or more, because, as he was wont to express it, he knew nothing better for the inside of a man than the outside of a horse. .

He was fond of horses and of dogs. One of my correspondents, who remembers Sir Henry and his family well, speaks particularly of the beautiful greyhounds he always had with him in the dining-room at Curzon Street. He took a pride too in his carriage horses, which were always fast, well-bred, and handsome. He drove very fast through the streets of London. Those of the West End, with which he was principally concerned, were far less crowded then than now; and I heard it said at the time, I know not how truly, that his coachman was always provided with Sir Henry's card, which in the event of a collision or other trifling accident he might drop and drive on, without pulling up or delay. Of the pains his friends took to supply him with a good riding horse, there is evidence in his correspondence.

He did not hunt, although Wistow is in the best hunting ground in England, in the Quorn district; neither did he shoot or fish. Whist, which he is said to have played well, was his favourite recreation. It was so from an early period, for I find in one of his earliest diaries, his whist account at Scarborough. There were few days in which he did not get a rubber, mostly at his club—the United University—of which he was an original member, in the evening and after his dinner. Perhaps in so doing he was acting on the sage counsel he once gave to a patient : " If you wish to preserve your eyes, never read by candle-light anything smaller than the ace of clubs." *

But Sir Henry Halford was not without his weaknesses and failings.   He was quick of temper and hasty of speech, but it was atoned for, by a prompt acknowledgment of his mistake, and he did not rest until he had made all the reparation that it was possible under the circumstances to do :

> " Of temper sharp and warm,
> Yet at his worst incapable of thought or wish to harm ;
> Too easily affronted, but as easily appeased." †

Or, as the Harveian orator of 1848, his friend Dr. Francis Hawkins, puts it : " Si forte dissensio aliqua incidisset, *quamprimum* redire in gratiam gestiebat animus."

It was a weakness of Sir Henry Halford to carry his courtly manners into ordinary life and society. This is to be regretted, for it was disliked by many, and it exposed him to ridicule and obloquy. ‡   But these manners were not

* *Temple Bar*, vol. xcvii. No. 386, p. 537.

† Lady Cork, " Memorials of Thought," p. 20.

‡ The " eel-backed baronet " is the sobriquet given him in

disliked by all his patients. One of them, Colonel Hawker, in 1835, writes thus : "Consulted on my case with Sir Henry Halford, the Prince and the Lord Chesterfield of all medical practitioners."*

So close an attendance as was that of Sir Henry Halford on the Royal Family, and so intimate a connection as was his with the court during the whole of the Regency and of the reign of George IV., could scarcely fail to influence the feelings, character and conduct of any man ; and considering the characteristics of the court at that time, it could scarcely be otherwise than adversely. Sir Henry was subjected to such influences for more than a quarter of a century, and this it was thought had given him too much of the feelings and habits of a courtier, to the prejudice of that

consequence of his deep and oft-repeated bows, by an acute and utterly unscrupulous contemporary, who elsewhere writes : "A flexible knee, a supple back, and a courtier's head have enabled Sir Henry Halford to carry on a thriving trade and to 'boo' his pretensions into the palace and into almost every nobleman's mansion in the kingdom." Mr. Bransby Cooper, in his "Life of Sir Astley Cooper," vol. ii. p. 222, tells us of Sir Henry's three profound formal bows to Lord Liverpool when he entered the room in which his lordship was lying on a sofa, utterly insensible, under the attack of apoplexy from the effects of which he eventually died.

* "Diary," vol. i. p. 283.

simplicity of character and sincerity which belonged to him in early life.

I know not how true this may be, and I prefer to dwell on points about which there is no dispute—on his services to the College of Physicians and his efforts to maintain the high character and social position of the English physician, on his scholarly attainments and on the marked success with which he practised physic. The confidence he inspired in his patients, the comfort he gave to them, his rare success in relieving pain and in assuaging the numerous other sufferings that attend on illness, and his fertility of resources in the gravest emergencies of medical practice—these were acknowledged and appreciated by his contemporaries and still survive in the recollection of a few. They are well expressed on the monument to his memory in Wistow church, as follows : " Ad morbos dijudicandos sagax, ad sublevandos pollens, ingenii acumine, remediorum copiâ pariter insignis."

Sir Henry Halford's only son, writing of his father in 1864, says, " There never was a kinder heart than his, never one more anxious to do justice to the merits of others, or more repugnant against inflicting injury or mortification upon any one." Testimony to the like effect was borne by all who knew him well and in the intimacy of his private and domestic life. The Duke of Rutland, writing on the 12th of March, 1844, to the second Sir Henry Halford on the death of his father, says:

"You will give me credit for all that I feel on the subject of the heavy loss which not you alone, but very many surviving friends have sustained, by the decease of your most excellent father. It is my hope that the event was so entirely foreseen by yourself and the family that its shaft was the less penetrating. I had been so long associated with your poor father by the ties of affectionate friendship, and I had had so many opportunities of knowing the amiable qualities of his heart and the extra-ordinary attributes of his mind, that I, more than most others, can appreciate and understand the extent of the calamity you suffer."

Sir Henry was very warmly attached to his brothers. To the younger of them, especially to the two who went into the church, he stood almost in the place of a father, making to them money gifts and loans as they severally needed them. To his father, to whom he and his brothers owed so much, and who had lessened his own resources for his old age by his liberality to them, Sir Henry contributed three hundred pounds a year from the commencement of 1802 to his death in 1813.

His pocket diaries show me that his charities were not infrequent and were of liberal, even of large, amounts.

Sir Henry Halford was ready at all times to do a kindness or service to any one who could prefer a proper claim upon him, and was never happier than when composing differences and paving the way to reconciliation between separated and opposed relations or friends, as witness some of the letters in previous pages.

A Greek Testament and a handy edition of Horace (the Glasgow edition of 1744, by Foulis, was his favourite) were always on his library table and within easy reach. To the last named of these, in preference to any other work, he was wont to turn whenever he sought to divert his thoughts from the routine of every-day professional work, and he was accustomed to declare always with satisfaction. He appears to have read nothing hastily or cursorily. Even on these occasions he read intently, dwelling on the thought conveyed rather than on the language in which it was expressed, though to the elegancies of this he was not indifferent—to use his own words: "it is a mistake and a perversion of learning when men study words and not matter, and fail to acquire something when they read, which they may fairly call their own."

He read a chapter, or portion of one, from his Greek Testament every morning; and it was his practice at Wistow to read a sermon, often one of Bishop Horsley's or Jortin's, to the family and servants on Sunday evenings. At Wistow he was a very regular attendant on the public services of the church; and he is said to have been so in London when his professional duties permitted. He had a warm sense of religion, and was an orthodox member of the Church of England.

Sir Henry Halford had succeeded in combining the character of the first physician of his age and country with that of the scholar and the country gentleman. The estimation in which he was held by his sovereign and at court, which in his case was the complement of his success as a physician, enabled him to render services to his profession, which its most distinguished members did not fail to appreciate. Moreover, Sir Henry

Halford attained steadily, yet rapidly, and without any perceptible extraneous aid, the largest practice and the most extensive reputation with the public; and he maintained the longest supremacy in both that has been known in this country. It is not to the interest of the medical profession to forget or to discredit such an example.

The object of these pages is to perpetuate the knowledge of so distinguished a physician, scholar, and member of society, and to rescue Sir Henry Halford's memory from the oblivion into which it was fast falling.

Printed by BALLANTYNE, HANSON & Co.
London and Edinburgh